ELLA AND THE ELEMENTALS

ANDREW S. FRENCH

NEONOIR BOOKS

Book three: Lost in America

Book four: Gone to Texas

Book five: The Final Girl

The Detective Jen Flowers series

Book one: The Hashtag Killer

Book two: Serial Killer

Book three: Night Killer

Book four: The Killer Inside Them

Northern Crime Fiction

Where The Bodies Are Buried

The Ophelia Red series

Book one: Ophelia Red

Crime Short Stories

Call Me: An Astrid Snow Short Story

Dark Snow: An Astrid Snow Short Story

Bette Davis Eyes: Detective Flowers Short Story

Go to www.andrewsfrench.com for more information.

1 HAPPY HOUSE

This wasn't the first house Ella Finn had broken into. She was twelve years old, but knew enough not to leave any fingerprints behind. She pushed her arms through the gap, squeezing into the window and dropping into the sink. Around her neck was a butterfly chain, a present from her mother a week before her parents had vanished. Ella pressed it between her fingers as her bare feet plopped into the water. A chill ran over her toes and up her legs, rushing through her until it clutched at her heart.

She'd left her favourite socks outside, the yellow and black ones which made her toes look like little bees. Ella's hair was dark and messy, as brown as her eyes and untouched by a brush for at least four days. She stared across the kitchen, waiting for someone to catch her, even though she knew her aunt and cousins had left without her. But her uncle could be in the house, the mysterious George whom she'd met just the once when arriving north at the home of her only living relatives.

Ella's hands shook, her fingers shivering not from cold or fear. Two weeks and three days after she'd stopped taking her medication, the anxiety had returned. The pounding in her head matched the thump in her chest. She fought against all of it and thought of her mum and dad and how they'd disappeared six months ago. She needed her phone to find them. That's why she'd sneaked into the house, even after her Aunt Ida had forbidden her.

The only thing keeping her calm was the fact she'd brought a friend with her. But the tiny rat squirming on her shoulder was nervous. Ratter's whiskers stood on end as Ella climbed out of the kitchen sink. She crept across the floor, her feet dripping dirty water as the cold kitchen tiles added to the chill in her bones. She pinched her nose at the stink of the boiled cabbage sitting on the cooker. Her aunt had left the food, unwanted and forgotten, and as she stared at it, Ella wondered if she was cabbage in human form.

She stole into the corridor, her hand pressed against the wall and the paper decorated with flowers she didn't recognise. The sight made her think of her parents again and how her father always brought bright, fragrant blossoms into the house, so their home was one of vivid colours and beautiful smells. She closed her eyes and saw the vibrant reds and purples and smelt the roses and lavender. They returned her to another time, one not so long ago, but which seemed like a different lifetime. Then she opened her eyes to the Twist household's dull grey and its insipid smell of nothing.

Ella gazed at the frames on the wall, and her three horrible cousins glared at her. They appeared as grumpy in the photo as they did in real life. She had to leave this new family of hers. Finding the phone was a start, but she also needed cash to return to London. Ella had no money of her own, and her aunt wouldn't give her anything.

I can't find Mum and Dad if I'm skint.

Ella looked around the kitchen. She could take some-thing from the house to sell.

It wouldn't be stealing. They've given me nothing since I came here, and I know they're getting money from the council for looking after me.

Ratter licked at her neck.

If they catch me in here, I'm toast.

But she had no choice if she was going to find her mum and dad. Her parents had been scientists working for the government when they'd vanished. She'd wanted to tell her mum's sister about it, but Ida was colder than ice cream when social services had dropped Ella off at the house.

'To lose one parent may be a misfortune; to lose both looks like carelessness,' Ida had said.

It wasn't quite the greeting Ella expected, and things hadn't improved since.

Her hand stopped shaking and she breathed a sigh of relief. Her aunt and the three girls had gone into town, and she hadn't seen her mysterious uncle in over a week. But he might be anywhere, and Ida and the kids would return soon.

She felt like a scarecrow as she crept up the stairs, the pants and shirt baggy on her bony frame, clothes handed down from her older cousins. Her fingers slid over the rail-ing. Ratter snuggled up to her neck, the animal's nose twitching as she sniffed at Ella's hair. Ella couldn't talk to animals or control them, but she'd always had an unexplain-able closeness to them. Her mum had called it an affinity.

She stood outside her oldest cousin's bedroom. Ratter shivered on her shoulder.

'It's okay, girl, Dolly and the others aren't here. I'll find the phone she stole from me, and then we'll leave and search for Mum and Dad.'

The corridor had a smell of old feet and dead fish. Her

toes bristled against the shaggy carpet, her shoes abandoned outside after the incident which had led to her punishment. It was only dirt from the cliffs she'd accidentally brought into the kitchen. But Ida had scowled at the sight of it, and the stink. Ella had to admit it did pong. Her eyes darted around the landing.

What if my uncle's in the house?

The rat jumped off her shoulder and dashed into the shadows as Ella turned to the bedroom door. Smack in the middle of it was a sketch of a grinning skull, and the words KEEP OUT! She held her breath and put her fingers on the handle. As she did so, the floor creaked downstairs.

'Whooo,' Ella whispered as the noises inside her head drowned out the sounds of the building.

The creaking came again, louder this time. It made her pause outside the room. If she didn't do something soon, the trembling would return and she'd never find her phone. She reached out and placed her hand on the door. The metal of the handle turned her fingers cold.

It's only the house groaning.

The wind whistled between the rafters as she discovered her courage and pushed the door open. She scuttled inside and Ratter followed. The rat vanished under the bed while Ella looked around Dolly's room. It was as she expected it, the walls full of shiny posters of pop stars and television celebrities, and an enormous bed covered with dark sheets and fluffy pillows. The bedroom carpet was smoother than the one outside, like marshmallows against her feet. A bookcase held tiny porcelain figures of Disney characters, while opposite it was a table draped with teen magazines and a laptop.

She'd better not have taken the phone with her.

The oldest cousin had snatched it from her when Ella

was taking photos of the beach and the pier. It was pointless complaining to Ida about it; she had to get it back herself.

Ratter popped her head from under the bed as Ella made for the wardrobe. Ella pulled the doors open and stared at Dolly's clothes: every single thing - tops, shirts, trousers, skirts, dresses and jackets - lacked colour. It was like gazing into a black hole.

Nothing but darkness, just like her soul.

The phone wasn't there and she slapped the wall. She strode to the chest of drawers as Ratter climbed up the sheets and on to the bed. Ella scrunched her eyes as she searched through Dolly's underwear in the top drawer, then the socks in the second one. She sat against the bed in relief when she spotted the mobile in the last drawer.

The joy of finding it made her forgot the time as she checked through the photos. She hardly used the phone for calls or texts, but it contained the most important things in her life: the only images left of her parents. It also had the code to get into their research facility at Artemis labs.

She swiped past the pictures of the beach, of the house, of the Victorian pier, of the surfers, of the countryside and service stations from her journey north, until she found what she'd wanted. Ratter was back on her shoulder as the tears came. She didn't wipe them away, staring at her mum's smile, her dad fooling around in their garden, the two of them kissing when they thought she wasn't there, and then the last photo she'd taken.

Ella held the screen up to the rat.

'They're waving at me, saying goodbye before I went to school.' Ella climbed on to the bed. 'And then they vanished.'

She buried her head in the pillows.

Her sobbing came fast and loud, like giant waves against

her heart. The phone dropped to the carpet and Ratter bounded over the sheets. The rat snuggled up to her face and licked Ella's cheeks. Her breathing was quick and heavy, noisy enough in her ears she didn't hear the front door slam shut below. Feet stomped up the stairs as she dragged her head from the bed and jumped to the floor.

'Oh no,' she whispered as someone banged into the door.

Ratter fled under the bed as the handle twitched. Ella fell to the carpet, grabbed the phone, and rolled after the rat. She reached the dark as three sets of feet barged into the room. Ratter shivered near her nose as two lumps landed on the bed, pushing into Ella's back. It was impossible to move as the girls sat right on top of her. Dust swirled around her head and jumped over her face. Bits of dirt stuck to her lips, and she wanted to sneeze. She held her breath and wished the urge away.

'Let's see what you've got.' It was Dotty who spoke, the middle of the sisters.

Something small with hairy legs ran over Ella's hand. She flinched and killed the noise in her throat. As she swallowed something terrible, one cousin dropped a shopping bag on to the floor. Ella stared at the green bits of the plastic before its contents emptied across the carpet.

'I'm gonna movie it when you give it to her.' That was Daisy, the youngest at thirteen, a year older than Ella. 'She won't expect a pressie from us.'

The girls cackled like witches. A large hand with jumbo sausages for fingers scooped up the guts of the bag.

'Make sure you put the worst itching powder inside the gloves.'

It was the unmistakable growl of Dolly Twist, fifteen going on thirty-five. Dolly marched everywhere with an invisible sign around her neck which screamed KEEP AWAY.

'Ya think she'll ave it from us?' Daisy said.

The space under the bed shrank as the two younger girls shifted about. The springs under the mattress stuck into Ella's chin, the weight of her cousins pressing down on her.

'Of course,' Dolly said. 'We'll tell her it's a welcome to the family present.'

Ella struggled to breathe as they snorted laughter through their noses.

'We have to make her life hell, don't we?' Dotty asked.

'Make it a living hell.' Daisy's laugh sent a shiver down Ella's spine.

'What's that stink?' Dolly's feet were only inches from Ella.

'It ain't me.' Daisy jumped up. 'I never farted.'

Ella wheezed into the floor, the weight lifting from her as the youngest Twist pranced around the room.

'It smells like rat shit,' Dolly said.

Ella gripped her chest and looked for Ratter, but she'd disappeared.

'There's summit under the bed,' Dotty shouted.

Then Ella's bones turned to ice.

2 THREE LITTLE PIGS

Dotty jumped off the bed. 'I felt it poking me bum.'

'Well, girls, it looks like we've got ourselves a dirty rat in the house,' Dolly said. 'A great big barn rat.'

A thick hand thrust under the bed and grabbed Ella's leg, sticking long pink nails into her skin.

'Ahhhhh,' Ella yelled.

Dolly dragged her into the light, picked her up by the back of her top and held her off the floor. Ella waved her hands around like a windmill, missing Dolly's face by inches. She twisted in the air, struggling to breathe as she avoided smacking into the wardrobe.

'What do we do with rats, girls? We throw them out with the rest of the rubbish.' Dolly laughed and dropped Ella on to the carpet with a thump.

'Ouch.' Ella squirmed on the rug and pushed her back against the closet.

Dust fell from the wood and drifted up her nose. It stank of old pyjamas. She forgot about her safety, eyes darting around to see if Ratter was okay. She could handle herself against them, but there was no telling what they'd do if they saw the rat.

'Are you going to cry, Smella?' Dolly glared at her.

Ella kept calm, digging her nails into the rug. She scanned the room, calculating how she'd get out unharmed, and scowled at her cousin.

'Your brains wouldn't fit into a thimble, Dolly.'

Daisy poked her in the arm. 'Watcha doing in ere, Smella?'

Ella wriggled against the wood behind her. She wanted to fall inside the wardrobe and disappear into another world; to do anything to get away from this family. She touched the back of her head, grimacing at the bump growing there.

'I'm returning your nose, Daisy. I found it in my business.'

Dolly peered at the device in Ella's fingers. 'She's nicked my phone.'

'That's a lie,' Ella said. 'It's my mobile.'

A fire burned in her blood as her leg ached from where Dolly had grabbed her. She gripped the phone as Dolly lunged and snatched at her hand. Ella rolled on to her side towards the underside of the bed and stared into Ratter's petrified face. If the cousins saw the rat, they'd kill her.

As one of them pressed against Ella's legs and Dolly clawed at her, she relaxed her grip. The older girl seized the mobile and the others let her go.

'What's so special about this, anyway?' Dolly said as Ella scrambled to her feet. 'You've got nobody to call or text because no one likes you, Smella.' She peered down at her. 'Are your eyes all blurry with tears?'

Ella scowled at her. 'No, my vision's fine. It's just unlucky I have to see you lot every day.'

'Maybe she fancies a boy at school?' Dotty said.

Ella grimaced while the others giggled.

'Who'd fancy a snot rag like er?' Daisy nearly choked on her laughter.

'Give it back.' Ella bared her teeth.

Dolly ignored her and scrolled through the screen.

'You've been taking snapshots of the town like a silly tourist.' She glanced through the photos. 'And we thought you hated moving from London to little old Saltburn, didn't we, girls?'

Ella lunged at the bigger girl who met her with a slap, knocking her backwards. Her cheeks were on fire, her skull searing in volcanic lava.

'Give it back, Dolly.' A thousand tiny needles burst inside Ella's head.

'Oh wait, now I see why you want this.' Dolly waved the phone in the air as Ella fumed. 'How sweet, your little collection of family photos. Look, girls.' She handed the mobile to Dotty, who showed it to Daisy. They sniggered together.

'Aunt Gemma had a funny face.' Dotty passed the phone back to her older sister. 'Not pretty like Mama.'

'Yeah, you don't need these pics filling up your storage, Smella. Let me get rid of them for you.' Dolly placed her thick thumb on the screen.

Ella stared at her. 'If you do that, you'll delete all the data on your phone.'

Dolly looked confused. 'What?'

'I linked it to your mobile and synchronised all the files. Anything you do to my phone will happen to yours.' Ella clenched her fingers.

Dolly turned to her sisters. 'Is that possible?'

Daisy and Dotty shrugged and pursed their lips in

stereo. Dolly's face grew redder and redder, looking like a giant tomato ready to explode. She threw the phone at Ella, who caught it before it knocked her eye out.

'You'll pay for that, squirt.'

Dolly cracked her knuckles and strode towards the bed. Ella was readying herself for the attack when the bedroom door burst open.

'What's all this ruckus?'

Steam billowed out of Ida Twist's mouth and ears. Her eyes bulged like a bullfrog, so her face wasn't so pretty now. Ella slipped the phone into her back pocket.

'Ella broke in to steal our stuff, Mama,' Dotty said.

Mrs Twist stared at her children one at a time before turning her gaze to the lodger in the family.

'Your mother would be ashamed of you.' She looked at Ella like a stern school teacher, her scowl transforming her face into a storm cloud. 'I forbade you to enter the house if I wasn't here, and yet you snuck in like a dirty thief. Go to your room. We'll talk about this tomorrow.'

Ella didn't need telling twice, jumping down and running out. She sprinted off and was outside when the shouting started upstairs. She grabbed her shoes and ran for the barn. When she got inside, she headed towards the far end as the wind howled across the cliffs.

Ratter's chirpy face greeted her from the bed.

'At least you're safe.'

She fell next to her friend and reached for the electric radiator. Uncle George had left it on one of his rare trips back to the Twist home. Even in summer, the barn was cold at night. The horses were at the far end. Ella loved the way they smelt, an aroma of sunshine, and sweat, and dirt; an adopt me and love me kind of smell. In front of them was the space George had set up as her living room: a small bed, lamp, heater, plus a metal stand where she put her books. She wasn't disappointed when her uncle told her she couldn't live in the house with the others. Being on her own was okay, and that was before she found out how horrible her cousins were.

Ella reached into her pocket and pulled out the cheese she'd taken from the kitchen. She bit into it before putting the rest in her palm and offering it to Ratter. As they nibbled at the food, Ella's thoughts returned to her situation. She'd regained her phone and got the better of her cousins. She had no money, but she'd think of something, would get the bus or the train to London, go to her mum's lab and search for her parents. They must be somewhere; people couldn't just vanish into nothing.

She'd visit her best friend, Lara Crawley. They'd met at school, and Ella had loved spending time with Lara and her sisters on their farm.

Lara was clever. She'd help Ella track down her missing parents.

First, she had to get away from here.

'Would you like to live in another city, Ratter?' They finished the cheese together as her tiny friend's eyes glistened in the gloom. 'We need to run away from here.'

———

THE RUNNING CAME SOONER than she expected. At eight the next morning, Ella scrambled near the cliff edge as the three little pigs chased her. She'd been up just before seven for half an hour of chores, dusting and hoovering downstairs. Breakfast was cold scrambled eggs and the bacon she ignored. Ella had lost count of the times she'd told her aunt she didn't eat meat.

'Are ya gonna scran that?' Daisy eyed the bacon.

'Be my guest.'

Ella got up and headed for the door, pausing when she noticed the hard rain hitting the window. The conditions seemed like the middle of winter, not the summer.

'The weather's been funny all year.' Ida sipped her coffee. Its aroma made Ella's nose wrinkle. 'But it's got worse these last few weeks.'

'It's ever since she turned up.' Dotty spoke through a mouthful of fried egg as she pointed at Ella.

'She's a jinx.' Daisy stuck her tongue out at Ella.

Ella stared at her cousins as they shovelled bacon into their mouths. They were like human garbage disposals chomping away at everything in their reach.

'Don't you feel like cannibals?' Ella said to them.

The cousins grunted together as Dolly lunged forward. Ella ran out the door and headed towards the sea, fifty feet below her. She ignored the warning signs along the edge of the cliffs, moving away from the house. She expected the girls to give up after a minute, but they kept on coming. Something wailed above her and added extra gasoline to her legs.

The rain and wind matted Ella's hair to her face so it swam across her head. One cousin was close behind, her fiery breath burning into Ella's neck. Long fingernails clawed at Ella's shoulder as she stumbled through the mud. She was younger than the others, but she was also faster, scampering forward and out of their reach as she pushed wet locks from her eyes. She'd never travelled this far along the cliffs before, but the next village was half a mile in the distance.

'Smella!' one of them shouted behind her.

Ella twisted her head to the side as she kept running.

Ratter's little body thumped against her chest inside her jacket. Her feet were like glue in the mud, struggling to move fast enough from the grunting girls. The rain softened to drizzle on her face, but the wind shrieked like a banshee. It blew her closer to the edge and the fatal drop to the sand below. Only last year a storm threw a kid from the cliffs and into the water. They still talked about it at school.

'We're gonna throttle ya.' Daisy's voice cut through the air.

It was hard to breathe with nature battering her lungs as Ella's legs turned to lead. She saw the drop to the beach and wondered if she could climb down before they reached her.

Someone knocked her to the ground before she could move any further.

'Now we've got you.'

Ella's lips kissed wet dirt as her shoulder throbbed. Dolly dragged Ella's arm and spun her on to her back. She stared at them through dark eyes, with her cheeks puffed out like fat balloons. The three of them glared at her. Raindrops bounced off her head and dripped into her mouth. She spat the water out and scowled at them.

'You're brave when you're together.' Ella wiped her lips. 'I'll take you one at a time.'

The rain stopped and the wind vanished as her insides turned into a shrieking kettle.

'Smella, Smella, yer going to Hellah,' Daisy sang as she skipped around and kicked Ella in the legs.

Apart from the crazed singing, everywhere was silent, as if nature had stopped to observe the drama on the cliffs. It was Dolly's gruff voice which broke the quiet.

'Poor Ella. She threw herself off the cliff because she was heartbroken by her parents' disappearance.'

'Whaaat?' Ella stuttered.

Daisy pressed her foot into Ella's ankle, digging the toe of her boot into the bone. Pain burst up her leg like jagged glass biting at her flesh.

Dolly grinned at her. 'And everyone hated her at school. So the lonely kid flung herself off the cliffs.'

Daisy laughed. 'Like that brat last year.'

'Why are you doing this?'

Ella struggled against the older girl's grip, nails burrowing into the dirt and scraping through the ground as Dotty got hold of her other arm and pulled her towards the drop.

Daisy threw clumps of grass at Ella's face. 'When yer gone, we'll ave all your dosh.'

'What do you mean?'

Ella spat out the words through the dirt in her mouth and kicked against her cousins to no effect. The edge was getting closer, the sea drifting up, all salty and damp and trying to dive between her lips.

Dolly pushed her fingers into Ella's arm.

'Why do you think Ma took you in?' Dolly snarled at her. 'It wasn't because she loved your mum. She hated her.'

Ella went limp in Dolly's grasp, heart thumping and head banging at those words.

'You're lying.' Water seeped into her shoes.

'You're valuable, squirt, and you didn't even know it.'

Dolly pulled again and Ratter trembled against Ella's ribs. She clutched at her clothes, trying to let the little rat go but failing as her cousin dragged her across the grass and mud.

'Yer ma left you a fortune,' Daisy said.

'But you don't get it until you're thirteen,' Dolly added. 'But our ma will get it if you have an unfortunate accident.'

'And we'll have our share,' Dotty said.

They were at the edge, the waves crashing below and echoing through Ella's ears. Her legs were lead as electric pain ran down her arms. She tried again to stand, but it was useless. She closed her eyes and remembered the last time she saw her parents waving goodbye.

Her mother's final words sang inside her head.

We'll see you soon, Ella.

The waves crashed against the sand below as her leg slipped out of Dolly's hand and dangled over the cliff edge.

3 THE BOOK OF ALL LIFE

A loud roar filled Ella's head, bouncing off the sides of her skull as if a train was screaming through her brain. She assumed it was from the sea until she realised it was coming from the sky. She peered into the air as a long dark wave approached. It startled the cousins and Dolly stumbled from the edge and into the grass, releasing Ella, so she scrambled backwards as the sound whooshed above them.

'Ahhhhh,' Dotty and Daisy screamed together, their hands above their heads as the flock of seagulls swooped down.

Ella rolled to the side as Dolly hit the earth with a whack, up and running before the birds came in for their second assault.

'Are you safe, Ratter?'

Ella stared at her friend as the rat peaked out of the inside pocket of her top. She squeaked when Ella glanced behind, and the seagulls flew off as the three little pigs staggered to their feet. She wasn't safe yet.

She slowed to catch her breath, and the wind brushed

the damp from her face. Her heart thudded against her chest and vibrated into her head as the cousins gained on her. Ella pushed the ache from her legs and stumbled forwards. Wet grass clung to her as she ran as fast as possible, the sea air sweeping into her nose and lungs. There was a taste of fish on her lips and the screams of teenage girls in her ears. There should have been a path across the narrowest part of the cliffs, but she couldn't see it.

Damn, damn, damn.

Ella clutched at her beating chest, her eyes resting on the sign saying DANGER: PATH CLOSED FOR RENOVATION.

She slid through the mud and pebbles to the edge, staring fifty feet down at a straight drop. She couldn't climb down that. Behind her, the sound of shouting grew closer. Her shoulders sagged as she faced her cousins, surprised at the sight of a massive house which hadn't been there before. Its many windows made it look like a giant fly towering over her, dark wood shimmering in the wind and sending a shiver down her spine.

'Damn!' she shouted as Daisy screamed so loud, it hurt Ella's head.

She ignored the shock, found the last bit of energy in her legs, and sprinted towards the house. No matter how scary it appeared, it had to be safer than what was chasing her. She threw herself against the door and fell inside. The floor was solid wood, but it was like soft foam when her body hit it. The entrance closed behind her as she made sure she didn't squash Ratter.

She scrambled to her feet, expecting her cousins to follow any second, but nothing happened. Ratter jumped to the ground and ran around in circles. The room was gloomy and smelt of old paper and burnt trees.

'Are you okay, Ratter?'

Ella crept towards the window as Daisy and her sisters gathered outside the house. Ella pressed her head against the glass.

'Where did she go?' Dolly yelled.

'There was an ouse ere,' Daisy said. 'She ran inside.'

'Don't be stupid.' Dotty scowled at her. 'There's nothing here.'

'Don't call me stoopid.'

Daisy shrieked and lunged at her sister. The two girls fell to the grass and clutched at each other's hair. Ella put a hand over her mouth as she giggled.

'Behave!' Dolly shouted as she scooped her sisters up like one of those grabbing machines you find in an arcade. She glowered at Daisy. 'Did she fall off the cliffs?'

The youngest Twist shook her head, looking confused. Dolly dropped them both.

Daisy shivered as she spoke. 'I swear, Dolly, there was a big spooky ouse ere, and she ran inside. It was all dark and scary, like in a orror movie.'

Dolly strode towards the window and Ella flinched backwards. Her heart smacked against her ribs as she stifled the gasp in her throat.

'She's crazy, Dolly,' Dotty said. 'Isn't she?'

Dolly was so close to the house, her breath caught on the glass. Ella moved forward and pressed her nose against the window. A barrier separated them, but Ella wasn't sure if it was the glass.

'There's something funny going on here.' Dolly peered straight into Ella's face. 'If the squirt fell off the cliff, they'll find her body soon, and we'll all get our share of the dosh.' She turned back to her sisters. 'We need to go to school now. Tell no one what happened here. We haven't seen Smella since she left the house, you got that?'

They nodded and followed their sister as she stomped off. Ella sighed as they disappeared in the distance. She moved from the window to check the rest of the building.

What is this place?

She looked for Ratter. The little animal had stopped chasing her tail and was crouching in terror against the opposite wall. Ella strode over and picked her up.

'You can feel it, can't you, girl? Something's off about this house.' She cradled the rat in her palms and scanned the entire room. 'Where's the staircase?'

She'd dashed inside, but remembered from the outside there had been two floors with an attic. There wasn't now. Dust lay everywhere like dandruff as Ella sneezed and scratched at her eyes. The house smelt like unwashed clothes stuffed into a basket. There was one room with no other doors apart from the one Ella had fallen through. The only furniture was a withered table standing against the wall. A large box sat on top of it. Something in Ella's head told her to leave, to run away from the strange house, but she ignored it. The worst that could happen to Ella had already occurred. This weird house couldn't harm her after that.

Let's see what's inside the box.

Ella opened her jacket and placed Ratter in a pocket, then walked to the end of the room. The box appeared to vibrate on the table and she hesitated in touching it. Ella breathed in and sucked up her courage. She pressed her fingers under the lid and lifted it, expecting a crazed jack-in-the-box to leap out at her. Ella sighed when nothing happened. She peered into it, surprised to see a book resting there. She pulled it out.

It was petite enough to fit in her palm, and the cover was antique leather, which felt like a pet tortoise she used to have. Tiny images covered the front and back. Ella didn't recognise many of them, but some she did. There was a unicorn next to a sphinx, and a witch on a broomstick flying above a sea serpent. It was exciting to see the pictures, and it made her wonder what was inside, but she was disappointed when she opened it and stared at the pages. They were all blank. The paper wasn't fresh, but a faded white turning to yellow, and it smelt like old shoes. Ella remembered her mother bringing ancient papers home from work and saying someone had made them from - what was it? Forgetting the word annoyed Ella. Pap something. Pappymus. No. Papyrus, that was it.

Ella wiped a tear from her eye and slipped the book into her pocket. She had to get to school.

'Come on, girl.' She allowed Ratter to climb on to her shoulder. Ella placed her hand on the door. 'I'll return later.'

She stepped outside, expecting the house to disappear when she closed the door, but it didn't.

Something doesn't feel right.

Ella stared at the sun burning bright in the sky. The ground which had been damp when she'd tumbled inside was now dry and crisp. The rain and wind had vanished, replaced by scorching heat which burnt Ella's face. She slipped into the shadows of the house and checked her phone for the time.

That's impossible.

She guessed it had been around eight-thirty in the morning when she'd stumbled into the mysterious house.

I was only inside about thirty minutes.

The time on her mobile was twelve-thirty.

'I'm late for school, Ratter.' She stared at the building in amazement as her brain worked out the unbelievable maths. 'Half an hour inside is four hours out here.' Ella shook her head. 'Maybe this is all a dream.'

She gazed into the distance, wondering where her cousins were and if they'd bully her later. Of course they would.

There's no point going to school.

Ella stepped back into the house and it was as before. Nothing had changed as she strode to the box and opened it. It was empty. Ratter jumped from her shoulder and ran to the centre of the room, seeming less confused than last time. Ella put her phone on the floor to watch the clock.

'Let's see what happens after another half an hour.'

Ella removed the book from her pocket. She opened it, expecting nothing, arching her eyebrows at the little illustration in the top corner of the first page. That wasn't there before. At least, she didn't think it was. She held it close to her face and squinted.

'It looks like a chubby butterfly with horns.'

'Don't be fattist,' a squeaky voice said behind her. Ella fell sideways as her elbow hit the floor. She stared in astonishment as Ratter spoke again. 'You have much to learn, Ella Finn.'

She righted herself and sat opposite the rat. 'You're not Ratter.'

The rat's eyes sparkled. 'Most of your kind have forgotten the likes of me, but your ancestors called us Sprites. I'm one of many Elementals. My name is Fazzlepuff.'

Ella couldn't help herself and giggled. She grabbed hold of her ribs and forced the laughter to stop.

'You came from the book.'

'You're smart, I like that,' Fazzlepuff said. 'And you'll

need those brains in the coming days and weeks, but you're not right. I'm from the other side. The book is the doorway which allowed me to inhabit your little friend.'

'Is Ratter in pain?'

'She's fine, but I can't stay in this form for much longer. Her body isn't firm enough for my Light. There are things I have to tell you before I return to the Elemental realm.'

Ella pulled at her cheek. 'Is this all in my mind?'

The rat scratched her whiskers and wriggled her nose.

'I promise you, it's real. You discovered the Book of All Life, and you must learn how to use it to prevent the catastrophe your kind has brought upon the world.'

'My kind?'

'Humans.'

'What have we done?'

Ratter's eyes sparkled. 'Humans have ruined everything. It's up to you to save the planet from climate change.'

'Me?'

'Yes. You. You're the only one who can stop the disaster that's coming.'

4 ILLUMINATION

The shaking returned to Ella's hands. She kept her legs steady; otherwise, she'd have ended up on the floor in a heap.

Fazzlepuff continued.

'How many images do you recognise covering the book?'

Ella took a deep breath. Her arms settled as she ran her fingers over the soft leather.

'Less than half.'

'There are thousands of different Elementals. Born out of Light and needing Light to live.'

Even though the Elemental was speaking through Ratter, Ella knew it wasn't talking about normal light.

'What is Light?'

The rat scuttled closer. 'All creatures are born with Light inside them, but it's most potent in humans. It grows stronger as you develop into children, but fades as you become adults. Some keep their Light through their love for others or the kindness in their hearts. For most, it disappears, and they feel empty without knowing why.'

'Like a spirit or the soul?'

'I don't know about human concepts, but Light creates and sustains life. All living things come from Light.'

Ella stared at the front of the book, peering at the small illustrations. She gazed at the image of a dragon.

'Are there good and bad Elementals?'

'You are a wise child. The good Elementals seek the Light of love and kindness, of compassion and companionship from humans, but the bad Elementals...'

'Want to hurt people?' Ella finished Fazzlepuff's words.

The rat's eyes grew wider. 'They want to consume humans, children in particular, to gather up the Light.'

Ella shivered and stared at the book. 'But dragons and witches and unicorns and all the rest don't exist.'

She peered across the mysterious house. Fazzlepuff let out something similar to a laugh, all squeaky and high pitched.

'We all exist on the other side of the veil, banished there many years ago by clever humans, our lives recorded in the book you hold. Men used the strength of nature to cast out the unnatural, but now nature is weakened in the air, in the sea, and in the ground, and gaps are appearing.' Silence engulfed the room and a chill invaded Ella's heart. 'Soon, the fissures will expand, and the most dangerous Elementals will arrive. Only the holder of the Book of All Life can send them back.'

Ella gasped, fingers trembling once more. She caught the book before it dropped to the floor.

'I...I...don't know what to do with it.' Her mouth was dry.

Fazzlepuff jumped on to her lap and she laid out her palm for the rat to sit in.

'I must leave now, but somebody is coming to guide you

with the book, someone from far away. You must return to your world before people miss you.'

Ella glanced at the phone to see another half an hour had passed inside the house. It meant it was four-thirty outside.

'Who is going to help me?'

The rat's feet warmed her hand. 'You'll discover that yourself. Now I must return to the Elemental realm.'

The spark vanished from Ratter's eyes.

Ella slipped the book into her jacket and Ratter into her pocket, got up and strode to the door. She stepped outside and ran towards home.

Fresh energy powered her legs and lungs as she sprinted past the dog walkers and the ramblers. Her aunt would punish her for missing a day at school, and there were the cousins to deal with, but Ella didn't care. She had the book, and she'd discovered that magical creatures existed. Trouble was brewing, but somebody was coming to help her, and she liked that. If her cousins bothered her again, she had a plan for them.

The Twist home appeared ahead, reigniting thoughts about her cousins and what they would do to her. The shudder snaking down her spine gave her an idea.

I can get food and water and hide in the mystery house until my mentor arrives. I could stay young in there while my terrible family grow older.

For the first time since her parents' disappearance, Ella felt happy.

And maybe I could use this book to find Mum and Dad.

Joy spread through her as she burst into the house and braced herself for Ida's telling off.

'You've been a naughty child, Ella, and I've come home to set you right.'

She stumbled into the back of a chair and stared at Uncle George. Her hands trembled on the wood as the fog drifted over her eyes. She wiped at them and struggled to breathe.

'What?'

'Sit down, Ella. This will take time.'

He wore a smart blue suit, a perfect white shirt and a skinny black tie. His dark brown eyes resembled pinholes at the bottom of a well. His head was bald, so he looked like a giant egg. Ida's face was a block of ice. Ella sat as Ratter shivered inside her jacket.

'The school has been in touch to say you didn't attend today. Where were you?' George rested his hands on the table. His nails were long and dirty.

'I wasn't feeling well, so I went to the beach.'

She wouldn't tell them about the mystery house and the book. They'd take it from her, and she'd never see it again.

'You were at the beach all day?' George replied.

'My stomach was terrible.' Ella stared at him.

He squirmed in his seat and coughed.

'You should've returned home immediately. You can't just sit in the sand if you're not well, child.' He peered right through her. 'Your aunt tells me you've been stealing from your cousins and being disruptive in the house.'

'They're lies!'

Ella shouted and glared at him. Her boiling blood destroyed her nervousness, her nails digging into the table, eyes about to pop from her face. She didn't want to stay calm, wanting them to witness her anger.

'And you've been talking back to your betters. This all stops now I'm home.'

He reached down to his side for something she couldn't

see. He grunted as he brought it on to the table. It was a cage full of straw.

Ella turned her hands into fists and stared at him.

'You want to move me out of the barn and put me in there?'

She pointed at the cage. Ella remembered being inside the mystery house, recalled talking to the Sprite as it told her about the Elemental world existing next to this one. It didn't matter what her terrible family did to her because she had a greater purpose than all of this.

George lifted from the chair and towered over her. A fire blazed through his eyes.

'You've brought vermin into the house.'

Ella cringed backwards. She wasn't scared for herself, but he could hurt Ratter.

'I haven't.'

'You can put the rat in here now, or I'll take it from you and snap its neck.' His voice was like dry poison. Ella gasped and slid back into the chair. 'I know you have it with you. I can see it breathing in your clothes.'

He marched to the side and reached out to her. Ella quivered, unsure what to do. She froze as he placed his hand inside her jacket and grabbed Ratter.

'Noooo,' Ella shrieked and snatched at George's hands. He squeezed Ratter between his fingers and pushed Ella against the wall. She screamed as he dumped Ratter in the cell. 'Leave her alone.'

She lunged towards Ratter in the prison. Before she reached her friend, Ida got up and stood between them. Ella couldn't do anything but howl in frustration. She fell to the floor and bumped her shoulder into the fridge. Shock rippled through Ella, her body trembling on the tiles.

Her uncle loomed over her. 'If you behave and do as

you're told, the rat stays in the cage and lives. If you don't, I'll feed it to Winston.'

'Who?'

Ella smelt the unknown creature before she saw it, its aroma drifting up to her nose as the bulldog strolled into the house. It pressed its wet face against her head. The hound growled as she stood and returned to the table. She struggled to breathe, a lead weight against her chest as she stared at Ratter in the cage.

'Do we have a deal?' George returned to his seat. Ella controlled her tears and nodded. 'Good.' He grinned like a clown. 'I left a perfect job to return here. Do you know what a petrochemical company is?'

'No.' Ella's lips trembled.

'Well, I was in charge of constructing a lucrative pipeline in the Antarctic. I've sacrificed that to return and look after you. So you better be grateful.' There was venom in his words.

Ella wiped away her tears and stared at Ratter's shivering body.

'You're the one damaging the world.' The fire returned to her eyes.

'What?' His face turned bright red.

She gripped her knuckles and shouted at him.

'You and the others poisoning the air and the ground and the sea with your chemicals and your greed. I should let the monsters gobble you up.'

All she could think about was bringing dragons and vampires there using the book. And they could deal with her horrible aunt and uncle. And then she'd get an Elemental to find her mum and dad.

George and Ida stared at each other for a few silent seconds. She expected them to tell her off, but instead, they burst out laughing. She blew out hot air as they laughed at her.

He stood and wiped the tears from his eyes.

'Your aunt will deal with you now, but you remember our agreement.'

He grabbed the cage and left. Ida stared at her, so Ella glared back. She pressed against the book in her pocket, so angry these stupid people were interfering with her mission. She couldn't save the world and find her parents without saving Ratter first.

'You remind me so much of your mother at that age.' Ida filled the kettle. 'She was clever and wilful like you, always getting what she desired.' She slammed the kettle down as she poured coffee into a cup. Ida didn't offer Ella a drink.

'Mum never mentioned you to me.'

Ella's breathing returned to normal. Pain stabbed at her heart once more at the mention of her mother.

'I was the older child, the one who should've had the support to go to university, but she was the one with the big brain good at maths and science. She was the one who ate up the family finances while she got her qualifications and training, and I was stuck at home living off the bare minimum. It was always "Gemma's good at this" and "Gemma's perfect at that". All in the expectation she'd get some well-paid job and repay our parents. But do you know what happened when she finished university?'

Ida finished her rant as the kettle hit boiling point.

'No.' Ella focused on how she'd rescue Ratter and get them both to the safety of the mystery house.

'She worked for peanuts at a charity developing clean water for Africa. That's where she met him, your loser father, and we were all forgotten about. She wasted what we'd sacrificed for her while hiding money in some account.'

Ida looked like she was about to explode as she poured the boiling water into the cup. The smell of coffee wafted across the room.

'You're a liar, and I hate you.'

Ella stayed as calm as possible as Ida sipped on the hot drink and examined her niece.

'You can go to bed now, child, with no food. Just remember your uncle travelled across the world to deal with you and what will happen to that dirty rat if you don't behave.'

She scowled at her aunt as she moved the chair and left the house for the barn. She pushed through the door and slapped her hand on the wood. The place seemed even colder without Ratter as she headed to bed. Ella dragged the blankets close to her shivering body to stay warm.

She peered at the cobwebs on the ceiling.

I'll rescue you, Ratter, I promise.

She ducked her head under the covers and pulled out the book. Ella touched the small pictures again, feeling the witch's hat, the dragon's tail, and the mermaid's scales.

Ella knew what she had to do.

Then I'll find Mum and Dad and save the world.

5 SCHOOL

'You make sure you go to school today, Ella.'

Ida popped dirty dishes into the sink as Ella finished her food in a rush and nodded at her aunt. She gulped down the milk and dashed out to the barn. Both last night and this morning, she'd scoured every nook and cranny in the home and buildings connected to it, rummaging through drawers and cupboards, peering under beds and on top of wardrobes, but with no luck in finding Ratter.

Her eyes flickered as she grabbed the book from under the bed and left. Perhaps she'd return to the mystery house and open the book. She glanced around as she stomped her way to school.

Why should I wait for somebody to show me how the book works?

It was inside the pocket of her jacket as she strode through the school gates. She sighed. Who was she kidding? She didn't know what to do with it, and she'd got Ratter into trouble. She could ask a teacher for help, she supposed, if they weren't so busy all the time.

Two teachers peered at her, but she avoided them and slipped next to a gang of girls from the year below. They were chatting about some TV show and ignored her. She glued herself to their shadows as they entered the building. Ella kept her eyes down and headed for the classroom of her tutor group.

She slid into her seat. The ginger-haired boy with the missing front tooth gave her a wide grin, and she smiled back. She could never remember his proper name, but everybody called him Billy Pudding. It was something to do with where he'd been born before his parents moved to Saltburn.

'I have important news for you, children.' The voice was unexpected and drew Ella's gaze to the front of the room. Mr Parker, the form tutor, should have been standing there. Instead, it was the Principal, Mrs Collins, and an adult and kid Ella didn't recognise: newbies. 'Unfortunately, Mr Parker is ill.' The Principal spoke to the class without looking at them. Some kids wiped tears from their eyes, mouths wide open in shock, while others yawned and struggled to stay awake.

'A dog landed on his noggin,' Billy leant in and whispered to Ella. She screwed her face into an uncomfortable position. What did he say? 'One of the older kids told me,' Billy continued. 'A Chihuahua fell from the balcony of the flat above his, and hit him on the bonce. I'll happen it's true because he's in the hospital.'

'Your new form teacher is Miss Barkay,' Principal Collins said. 'And she's come to join us from Scotland. Do you children know where Scotland is?'

Heads nodded slowly.

'Do you want some chuddy?'

Billy held out his hand to Ella, offering her a piece of chewing gum which had seen better days.

'No, thanks.'

She itched to look at the book again, but stared at Mrs Collins instead.

'Good, children. Well done. And this is our other newcomer, Dora.' The Principal put her palm on the girl's shoulder. The kid was scraggy, smaller than most in the class, with dark hair resting on her shoulders, and unusual eyes. They were emerald green, and even from where Ella sat at the back, appeared to sparkle like stars in the night sky. 'Dora is from Greece. How many know where that is?'

There were blank stares everywhere.

'There's plenty of grease in me ma's kitchen,' some kid shouted.

The rest of the class collapsed into giggles. Even Ella snorted a little.

Dora shrugged the adult hand from her shoulder and pouted at the Principal.

'I'm not from Greece.'

'What?'

'My parents were from Greece. I was born here.'

Ella gasped at the stubbornness of the new kid. Nobody spoke back to Principal Collins, not even the other teachers. Collins had once made one of the dads in the playground cry like a baby when she'd blamed him for his son's constant bad behaviour.

'Okay, child; grab a seat where you can.'

The Principal lost interest and left as Miss Barkay took registration. Dora strode to the only empty chair available, those intense green eyes catching Ella's gaze as the school day got under way.

Ella's morning was one session of boring Design Technology, and her favourite class, double English. At lunchtime, she sat at the back of the dining hall, looking at the book. None of the other kids gave her a second glance. She ran her fingers over the cover, enjoying the way the illustrations tickled her skin, and checked inside the first page. The image of the Sprite had disappeared, but it was other creatures Ella was thinking about.

Imagine a world full of dragons and witches and sea serpents and goblins.

She was concentrating on the empty pages when Billy Pudding marched over and distracted her. Bits of fish were stuck to his teeth as he spoke.

'There's somethin I need to tell ya.'

He plopped into the seat opposite her, with mustard on his chin and fresh tomato clinging to his school jumper. Ella acknowledged his presence and scanned the hall for Dora. She hadn't seen the new girl all morning. What if the other kids were giving her grief? And she still didn't know how she'd find Ratter and get her free.

Perhaps I can use the book to find Ratter. Some magical creatures must be hunters. And then I could use it to find Mum and Dad.

Her heart soared at the thought.

Billy leant towards her. 'It's important.'

'What?' Ella finished her cheese pie.

'The Twist girls will jump you in the playground, right in front of the other kids.'

It didn't surprise Ella. She'd been waiting for something like this since escaping from them inside the mystery house.

'How do you know?'

His attempt to force a small potato between the gaps in his teeth mesmerised her.

'I overheard them talking about it in the corridor. They

used to bully me all the time until you arrived. They put me in a right flummox, they did. Picking on me because of my hair, or the way I speak, or these clothes.' He grabbed at the sleeve of his shabby jacket. 'I hate this uniform. Mum had to buy them from a charity shop.' He lifted his arm to his nose. 'They smell of old people.'

He pulled a chocolate bar from his trousers. It resembled a frog with a face too big for its body. He offered her some, but she shook her head. What he'd told her didn't worry Ella. If she were important enough to have the Book of All Life, she wouldn't let her cousins bother her.

Billy took bits of paper from his pocket and put them on the table. They were bright purple with a unicorn illustration on them, like the one on the book.

Ella pointed at them. 'What are those?'

'There's a carnival in town, and I won three tickets for it.'

She picked one up and read it out. 'The Carnival of Curiosities: gaze in astonishment at the Living Mermaid, Goblin Man, the Tiny Dragon and many more.' Ella's face lit up like a Christmas tree. 'Are these real?'

He wiped cream cheese from his nose.

'I dunno, but we could find out. Do you wanna go tomorra?'

Maybe the person coming to guide me works at this carnival if it has all these creatures.

She grinned at him. 'Definitely.'

The school bell rang for the start of lessons.

'What will you do about your relatives?' Billy shouted as Ella headed to class.

She didn't have an answer, but she spent all afternoon trying to think of one. When the last lesson finished, she waited in the room until everyone left, including the teacher. Ella wandered over to the window and stared outside. She couldn't see any of her cousins, but a large crowd of kids had gathered in the playground.

'Is school always this boring?'

Ella turned as Dora stood in the doorway, her emerald eyes shimmering.

'Yeah. I can't wait to grow up and stop being a kid.'

Ella didn't feel like a kid, hating how all the adults treated her.

Dora joined Ella at the window. 'What are you searching for?'

'An escape from school without getting my skull smashed.' She moved to one side, catching her jacket on the desk, and the book fell to the floor. 'Damn.' Ella scooped it up.

Dora gazed at it. 'Do you enjoy reading?'

'I do whenever I find something interesting.'

There was nothing to read in the Twist house unless you liked celebrity gossip magazines, and the school library was full of volumes which were years old. But at least she had some of her books in the barn.

'I read all the time because there's so much to learn.'

Ella nodded at her. 'I'm the same. Proper books, though, not stuff off the internet.'

Dora examined the volume in Ella's hand. 'That looks like a Grimoire.'

'What's that?' Ella's fingers moved across the images on the front of the book.

'It's an ancient collection of myths, legends and spells. My parents told me stories about one our family had in Greece.'

Dora reached out to touch the Book of All Life, and Ella didn't stop her. Something about Dora put her at ease, and she was desperate to tell somebody what had happened with the Elemental. Dora touched the front cover, running her fingers over an image of a giant dog with six heads and the illustration of a woman with snakes for hair.

'Do you believe in magical creatures?'

'Of course,' Dora replied. 'Apart from Santa Claus.'

They giggled together. Ella couldn't remember the last time she'd laughed with someone. Why should she care about those kids outside when she was making a new friend here?

She smiled at Dora.

'There's a carnival in town which might have magical creatures in it. Would you like to go with me and Billy Pudding after school tomorrow?'

After spending weeks when everyone either ignored or picked on her, Ella enjoyed the unusual idea of new friends.

Perhaps this has happened because I discovered the book and one of them will help me with it?

'Sure, of course. But what's a Billy Pudding and who's going to smash your head in?'

Ella's immediate problems came rushing back to her. She was going to reply when Billy burst into the room.

'Your horrible cousins are waiting outside to get you.' His eyes were on stalks. 'And they have a big gang with 'em.'

Her heart sank at Billy's words. Everything seemed quiet outside, but her fingers tingled. She pushed her hands against the glass and let the cold seep through her.

'Dora, this is Billy.' She stared at the boy. 'Where are the teachers?'

'There's a scrap in the sports hall, so they all went there.'

Dora put her hand on Ella's arm. 'Perhaps the book might help you.'

'How can that help me?'

She thought of the mystery house and the creature that had spoken through Ratter. Ella had the book to save nature, not to deal with her bullying cousins.

Dora looked at Ella. 'Only certain people understand how to use a Grimoire. If it's an enchanted book, perhaps you can use the magic to help you. Can I see at it?'

Ella hesitated before handing it over. Dora gazed at the front cover, but didn't look at the pages.

'All these creatures, and others, could do whatever you want.'

Dora's words made the hairs on her neck shoot up. Dora returned the book to her, and Ella clutched it to her chest, the illustrations pressing against her clothes.

If I'm going to save the world from climate change, I must act like a wizard. And a wizard can do anything.

Including blowing down three little pigs.

6 PLAYGROUND TWIST

Dora pointed at the cover. 'Perhaps a few small creatures might scare your cousins and the others.'

'Do you know how the book works?'

A loud noise exploded from outside. Ella peered through the glass as the group of kids increased in number. She couldn't leave school except through them.

Dora ran her fingers across the book. 'A Grimoire is a textbook of magic, with directions on creating enchanted objects like talismans and amulets and performing magical spells. It can also summon or raise supernatural creatures.'

Billy's eyes grew as wide as his head. 'Blimey, you're a reet clever clogs.'

'But this only has blank pages.'

Ella dropped her shoulders and stared at the floor. Maybe the ground would swallow her if she peered hard enough.

Dora shrugged. 'Perhaps it's more about following your instincts than focusing on instructions. Not everything you learn has to be taught.'

Ella buried her face in her hands, waiting for the shaking to start, thankful it didn't come.

'My only instinct is to leave this school.'

Her thoughts were like mush, wondering how she'd avoid the gang. If the cousins didn't get her now, they would when she returned to the Twist home. She had to rescue Ratter and hide out in the mystery house. Let them all get older while she waited for someone to help her with the book.

She gazed at Dora. Could her guide be this strange new girl?

'Close your eyes and imagine what you want to appear. The smaller the creature, the less you need to think about it. That's what my grandma used to say.'

'Flippin' eck, is that a magic book?' Billy's face was a picture of confusion, the boy struggling to keep up with the girls' conversation.

Ella scanned the images again. She ignored his question and turned to Dora.

'What's this?'

Ella pointed at the creature resembling a deformed faery. It had a massive head, bigger than the rest of the body, bushy beard and wrinkled skin. Its arms appeared longer than they should have been.

'That's a knocker,' Dora said.

Billy peered at the image. 'What's one of them?'

His face was close to Ella's, and she caught a strong whiff of liquorice and baked beans.

'It's an Elemental of the underground.' Dora squinted and furrowed her brows. 'They're supposed to be spirits of dead miners.'

'My da worked down the pits until they were all shut.'

Billy stared into the ceiling as he spoke about his father. 'He never mentioned seeing anything like that.'

'Are they good or bad?'

Ella wouldn't bring nasty creatures into the world, even if it was to deal with her horrid cousins.

Dora rubbed at her chin. 'From what I remember, they protected the miners from danger, but they are easy to anger. They're small creatures and don't like it when people laugh at their lack of height. You could fetch one here to scare those kids away.'

The shouting outside increased. Billy went to the window.

'There are dozens of 'em now. You'll never get through that alive.'

Ella turned to Dora. 'I just shut my eyes and picture this creature to bring it here?'

Dora nodded. 'Keep hold of the book and believe the knocker is real. Believe it with all your heart, Ella.'

Ella took a deep breath and gripped on to the book. She closed her eyes and imagined the Elemental marching through the playground. She concentrated for three minutes, but nothing happened.

Ella sighed. There was no magic in those pages. Or maybe she wasn't the right one to use it. It had been stupid to try and she'd been foolish to believe. She slipped the book into her pocket.

'Let's get this over with. They're only after me, so you two stay out of the way.'

Ella slumped out of the classroom and down the corridor. She opened the exit and stepped into the playground. Dora and Billy whispered to each other behind her. She noticed Billy giving Dora one of the carnival tickets as the crowd parted in front of her. Dora dragged Billy into the safety of the shadows as all the other kids ignored them. They were only there to see Ella's beating.

Dolly stood tall above everyone. 'About time you got here, Smella.' The surrounding kids giggled. 'You said you wanted to fight us individually, so now's your chance.'

Ella glanced around her, calculating how she'd get away from them with no trouble. As she did so, Daisy came bundling towards her, arms and legs waving like a windmill. She was slim and light but packed a punch when she caught Ella on the head. Pain shot through Ella's ear.

'Fight!' the kids screamed as Ella stumbled backwards.

Daisy continued, her hands raining on Ella's arms as she held them up in defence.

'I'm gonna batter ya.'

Daisy pushed Ella into the wall at the back of the kitchens. A whiff of fish fingers and cabbage covered Ella's face as Daisy rained blows on her. As she gathered her breath, Ella glanced down to see bits of food dumped there. She kicked the thing closest to her so it landed underneath Daisy's right foot. As Daisy stepped forward, the banana skin skidded, her ankle turned to one side, and she slipped. Her legs flew into the air, her body going upwards in slow motion before coming down with a crash like a cartoon come to life. It stunned the screaming crowd into silence.

'Fruit is good for you, cousin.'

Ella stepped over Daisy and towards the kids and the exit behind them.

'You won't get so lucky with me.'

Dotty blocked Ella's way. She put her fists up like a boxer and danced around Ella. Ella twisted her head as Dotty's right hand flew at her. But it was a feint by the middle Twist. She brought her left hand around and caught Ella on the chin.

'Argh,' Ella said as electricity burst through her face. She staggered sideways as Daisy bombarded her with a volley of punches with both hands, right and left into her stomach. Ella moved her head, coughing as she spat to the ground. She clutched at her gut as Dotty grabbed her by the shoulder. Dotty spun her around and threw her towards the howling crowd. Ella hit a bunch of them and fell to the concrete.

'Smella, Smella,' the kids shouted as they kicked at Ella. She curled into a ball as feet stamped on her legs and arms, pain rushing through her body. She pushed her head into the cold floor, but the chill couldn't settle the anxiety flowing through her bones. It was only the loudness of Billy's voice which distracted her.

'Geronimo!' he said as the children stopped kicking her and she peered upwards. 'Get away from her, ya manky brats.'

Billy swung a hockey stick above his head with enough force to propel an aeroplane into the air. The kids screamed and scattered. He kept on swinging with one hand while reaching down to her. Ella smiled at him and raised her arm.

She was about to grip him when a dark shadow fell over them. It grabbed his shoulders and threw him into the sky. He landed with a bang next to Ella.

'This has been fun, but we need to get home now and watch Dad squash your rat.' Dolly picked Ella up by the scruff of her neck. The older girl peered into Ella's eyes and smirked. Ella slumped in those chunky fingers as Dolly shook her like a tree in the wind. The book fell from her jacket and Ella gasped.

Dolly squeezed Ella hard. 'Have you been keeping more secrets from us?'

Daisy scuttled over and grabbed the book in her thin fingers. 'That's a pretty cover.'

'I didn't think you could read,' Ella said between massive coughs. She dangled above the ground as every bone in her body ached.

'There's nowt in it.' Daisy flicked through it. 'Apart from a picture in the front.'

Dolly glared at her sister. 'A picture of what?'

Daisy pushed her nose into the pages to get a better look.

'It's some ugly goblin thing.'

Ella continued to struggle as Billy groaned and stood. The gang of kids regained their bravery and crept closer to the action. Ella sighed as the mob yelled as one.

'It's a monster,' they cried together.

'What?' Dolly let go of her victim.

Ella blinked at the beast approaching them, wondering what it was until she realised it was the Elemental from the book's cover: the knocker. But it wasn't small enough to fit in a mine since it was bigger than Dolly, over six feet tall. Some kids screamed while others stood there and gazed at the strange creature. The knocker's hairy knuckles scraped across the ground as it let out a loud fart, sounding like someone bursting a balloon.

'Ahhhhh,' the gang shouted and grabbed their noses. Some of them sprinted off, but most stayed and gawped at the weird beast.

'You're an ugly kid,' Dolly said to the knocker.

Ella stared in amazement, with Daisy rooted to the spot in shock. Ella snatched the book from her hands and ran to her saviour.

'Get up, Billy.' She helped him from the ground.

'What's that?' He gaped at the knocker as it strode towards Dolly.

'It's an Elemental,' Ella whispered as Dolly threw a punch at it. She hit it right in the face and it didn't move an inch. It opened its mouth and blew foul-smelling green slime all over Dolly Twist.

'Ahhhhh,' the kids shrieked as they sprinted out of school.

Dolly jumped on the creature, pushing both of them to the ground. The action hypnotised Ella as the two of them rolled around the floor. Dolly punched away, but nothing seemed to faze the knocker. It belched, the sound louder than a rocket, the force throwing Dolly back. Then Dotty sprinted over and kicked at the beast.

Ella pulled Billy behind her as they fled, following the screaming kids. Ella didn't consider what would happen to the Twist girls. When they reached the school gates, Dora was waiting for them.

'It worked, then,' Dora said as the three of them sprinted away. They ran past houses and shops, across the road and into the trees.

'What was that?' Billy shouted between big gasps of air.

'I used the book.' Ella still ached, but a sense of joy compensated for that. The school was far behind them and she relaxed a little. They moved more slowly over another road and headed towards the sea.

'Where are we going?' Dora said as they reached the bank down to the beach.

Ella gazed at the sea. 'The tide's out. Let's hide near the pier so I can tell you something.'

They jogged down, Ella staring at the two kids she hadn't spoken to before today. Could she trust them with the secret of the book and the mystery house? Billy had risked himself to save her, and Dora knew it was a Grimoire, or something similar. Ella made her mind up to explain everything. Plus, she'd need assistance to rescue Ratter.

And they could help me find Mum and Dad.

They moved past the few tourists queuing at the fish and chip shop near the pier. Ella grabbed her new friends and gazed into their startled faces.

'There's a place full of magical creatures, and we'll bring some of them here to save the world.'

7 RAT TRAP

'Follow me.'

Ella ran past the fish shop, the arcade, the entrance to the pier, and the surf shops, dodging the tourists and heading under the pier. She jumped over bits of stone sticking out of the sand with the other two just behind her.

Billy slid in next to her. 'I'm jiggered.'

The sea air drifted up Ella's nose as the seagulls squawked above. She wondered if they were the same ones who'd saved her yesterday. She placed the book face up in her lap and told her new friends everything that had happened since the chase along the clifftop.

'That's all of it.'

'Flippin' eck.' Billy removed his blazer, the jumper dangling off him like a large blanket. 'It'd nark me off if they were my family.'

Dora gazed at Ella with sympathetic eyes. 'What happened to your mum and dad?'

Ella shifted in the sand as a tiny crab scuttled over the sand. Someone somewhere had turned the dial on the sun to the maximum as they shrank into the shade of the pier to escape the heat. Her fingers brushed against the silver butterfly symbol hanging around her neck.

'They disappeared. Where are yours?'

'They died,' Dora replied.

An awkward silence fell over the three kids. Behind them was the sound of surfers looking for waves as the tide headed towards the beach.

'You've got to show us this weird house.' Billy drew a shape in the sand with his fingers. When he'd finished, it was the unmistakable image of the knocker.

'I need to find Ratter first and rescue her from my uncle.'

Ella wiped the sweat from her forehead as Billy rolled up his sleeves. Dora was the only one not bothered by the growing heat. She grabbed a stick and pointed at Billy's sand drawing.

'That might help you. A knocker has a great sense of smell because of its giant nose. It can sniff out your rat friend.'

Ella and Billy stared at her in amazement.

'How do you know this stuff?' Billy picked a piece of fish from his teeth. Ella guessed it had been there since lunchtime.

Dora smiled at them. 'It fascinated my parents, this type of thing, myths and legends and fairy tales.'

Billy grimaced, his voice trembling. 'Won't it attack us?'

Dora shook her head. 'Ella can control it with the book.'

That didn't convince Ella. 'Why was it so big? You said they'd be a couple of feet tall.'

Dora shrugged. 'I don't know. Perhaps they've grown bigger since the mines were closed.'

'How do we get it here?' Ella stared at Billy's drawing.

Gulls swooped around them, squawking and cawing near the pier. Dora put her hand on Ella's shoulder.

'Place your finger on the picture. Imagine the creature travelling here, and it'll come to you.'

Ella hesitated before going to the page.

Maybe I should wait until the guide comes to teach me how to use the book?

She shook her head at the idea. It would be too late for Ratter by then. She went to the page and followed Dora's instructions. The drawing was soft on her skin as she thought about the knocker.

'Come to me,' she said as the other two watched her. The gulls disappeared, and silence engulfed them. 'Come to me.' Ella pressed her fingers further into the ink. Dora stared at her while Billy wiped more sweat from his face.

After three minutes, nothing had happened. Ella let out a loud groan. 'It's not working.'

Dora touched her arm. 'Give it time. The creature can't fly here.'

Billy cricked his neck to stare at the sky. As he did, something grunted behind them. Ella flinched and turned to see an enormous face with wide-open eyes watching her. Two huge teeth hung over its lips like a sabretooth tiger. Drool dripped from its mouth and on to the sand. It was close enough for Ella to smell its breath of rotten eggs.

'What a pong.' Billy squeezed his nose.

The knocker grinned at Ella as she pushed the book into her chest.

'Did he walk here?'

She had visions of people fainting in the street when they saw the Elemental striding by. The baking heat wouldn't help either.

'I guess so,' Dora said. 'Now we have to take him to your house if you want to find your rat.'

'Won't people say something?' Billy let go of his nose.

'I don't think so.'

Ella stood and held her hand out to the knocker. Her heart was beating at a hundred miles a minute and there was a shiver across the top of her flesh. The Elemental appeared as nervous as she was, stretching out his fingers with long yellow nails reaching towards Ella. They clasped, her smaller one wrapped inside his shovel of a hand, his skin like the bark of an old tree. He grunted as they marched from across the sand.

Billy wiped at his head. 'Why not?'

Ella glanced around her. 'People look different nowadays. We might get a few stares from some on the beach, but nobody will say anything.' She strode hand in hand with the creature underneath the pier, the waves lapping at their feet. The knocker snorted as he moved across the sand, his massive toes crunching through the orange earth. Dora stuck close to him on the opposite side to Ella while Billy kept a safe distance. A small pup ran at them through the water, its little legs pounding into the sea as it yapped and barked at the strange sight. The knocker paused, its gigantic eyes expanding even further to peer at the pooch. They glared at each other for thirty seconds before the dog yelped in fear and turned on its heels.

Billy laughed as Ella pulled the knocker with her. 'We need to take the gravel footpath near the pub.' They approached the building. 'The Twist house is at the top.'

The knocker clumped forward, dragging Ella behind him, his colossal nose twisting from side to side.

'Go find the rat.'

Dora ran beside them. Ella let go of his hand as the

knocker clambered up the path and headed away from the Twist home.

'Wait.' Ella tried to keep up. She kept her voice as quiet as possible so as not to alert whichever of the Twists might be at home. The Elemental dragged his knuckles through the mud, snorting spit on to the floor as he ran past the building and towards the cliffs. 'What's wrong?' Ella said to Dora as they scrambled to catch him.

'He's going to jump off the cliff,' Billy shouted as the knocker headed straight for the edge. Ella panicked, wondering what she'd done to make him like this.

She smacked herself in the forehead.

I should've waited for my guide to show me how to use the book.

She expected the knocker to disappear into the sea, cursing as she ran towards him, skidding through the grass and slipping to the ground. Ella grabbed his leg and his thick hair brushed against her cheek. He looked down at her, a grin creeping over his face.

'Nooooo,' Billy roared as the knocker jumped off the cliff with Ella clinging to him. Billy yelled again and ran to the edge. When he got there, he discovered the knocker hanging on to the side by one hand as Ella stared at the sea below. The wind battered her head as her heart thumped against her chest. She slammed against the cliff as the knocker grabbed the top of the grass. Ella's face pushed into the mud before she used her free hand to rub dust from her eyes and stare at the cage with Ratter inside. It sat on a ledge connected to two hooks in the earth.

'Are you okay, Ella?'

Billy knelt next to the knocker's head and held a hand out to her. Her breathing came in rapid bursts, sea air brushing past her nose as she took in a massive smell of salt.

'I'm fine,' she shouted through the wind. 'I'm going to rescue my friend.'

Ella clung to the knocker's leg with one hand, then opened the door and pushed her fingers inside the prison. Ratter climbed into her palm and she removed her from the cage. As she did so, the knocker lifted them on to the cliff and threw his legs over the edge. She rolled to the side, letting Ratter go so the rat could scamper through the grass.

Dora ran to her. 'Are you all right?'

Ella slumped on her back and laughed. 'That was exciting.' She grinned at the clouds hovering above.

Billy joined them. 'I thought you were a goner.'

'Me too,' Ella replied as Ratter nibbled at the grass. The three kids lay down and peered into the sky.

Billy held a hand towards the sun. 'What do we do now?'

The knocker grunted and sat next to them while Ella lay between the other two. She took their hands in hers, smiling at how she'd gained new friends.

'I can't keep Ratter here, or even with me. And we must do something with the knocker.'

She sat up and smiled at him with gratitude.

Dora stood. 'You can return him to the other side by erasing the image in the book.'

Ella puffed out her cheeks. 'How do I do that?'

'Put your finger over the drawing and imagine him going back.'

Ella got up and strode towards the knocker. She stretched up, threw her arms around him and whispered into his ear.

'Thank you, my friend. Now take some of my Light.'

She squeezed Elemental flesh and gave him her love. She hoped that's how it worked, but she didn't feel any different. After two minutes, she let go, stepped backwards, and took the book from her jacket. She opened it and put her finger over the illustration. She smiled at the knocker as he vanished.

Dora stared at her. 'I need to get home.'

'And me,' Billy added.

Ella thanked them both. 'We'll meet tomorrow morning at school.'

They went their different ways as Ella imagined George's expression when he discovered Ratter had escaped. She pushed the front door open, expecting to see Ida's scowling face, but the house was silent and dark. She flicked the corridor light on and stepped into the kitchen. The room was empty, and she was in no hurry to find the Twists. For a second, she wondered if the knocker had paid them a visit between the school and the beach.

If my thoughts brought it to the beach, maybe it could've heard what I was thinking about my cousins.

Then she noticed the note on the table. She picked it up and read it with a heavy heart.

We've gone to the hospital. Dotty is hurt. Ida.

Ella slumped into a chair and stared at the words. The knocker must have injured Dotty during the fight at school. Ella disliked the girl, but she didn't want this. She sat alone in the kitchen, her mind swamped with many things.

After thirty minutes, her stomach growled. She raided the kitchen to make a sandwich. When the Twists hadn't arrived home by ten o'clock, she closed the door behind her and went to the barn. She slipped the book under the pillow and let Ratter run free.

'Keep out of sight, girl, in case they come looking for us.'

It was near midnight when the car pulled up outside. She dragged the sheet over her head and pretended to be asleep. The barn door creaked and heavy footsteps strode towards the bed. A shadow crept over her as Ella gripped her beating chest.

She couldn't see who it was, but knew Dolly stood there.

'Dotty's in a coma and it's your fault.' Heat flowed out of her. 'I could snap your neck like a twig, but I'm going to make you suffer in front of the entire school. And it's going to happen soon.'

She smelt Dolly's breath through the sheets. The older girl lingered there for a minute before leaving. Ella poked her head out to ensure she'd left. When she was sure, she took the book from underneath the pillow and clutched it to her chest. Using it had saved her from her cousins and the other kids, but at what cost? She'd read about people in comas; it was rare they ever recovered. Dotty could be like that forever, and it was all her fault.

I can't use the book again.

She stuffed it under the bed, engulfed by sadness for the cousin who hated her.

8 THE OTHER

While Ella was hanging over the cliff edge to rescue her pet rat, an alarm rang in a large house in a small Irish town. It shrieked and Kylian Morrigan froze in shock, the tiny hairs along his arms shivering like alien tendrils.

He clutched the vibrating bracelet on his wrist and raced outside. The metal throbbed against his skin, sending warmth through his arm. He dashed over cobbled streets as the bangle returned to normal and he took the phone from his trouser pocket. Kylian swiped the device into life and found his contact list, pressing the top number as he sprinted. A group of kids not much younger than him kicked a ball around while dogs barked at his back. He turned a corner and headed to his grandma's place. It was colder than it should have been, even for a British summer, but it wasn't the chill which bothered him.

'I need to take time off,' Kylian spoke into the phone when the connection clicked at the other end. 'I'll text you the details later.'

Being employed as a takeaway food driver was not

something he'd ever classed as a career. What he was about to do now was what he'd waited all his life for. It was what all the training was about. There had been countless others before him, but he was the one who would face a date with destiny.

'Where are you, Gran?' He was inside as he shouted, striding by the shelves full of thimbles and into the living room. In the corner was an old piano looking like a recovery from a shipwreck. Half a dozen cats jumped up to greet him as he barged past them and into the kitchen. They scowled and shrieked as he went. The place stank of fried onions and grilled meat.

A woman with long white hair and skin like a tortoise sat at the table, her mouth on the verge of biting into a thick wedge of bread as Kylian spoke.

'Somebody opened the door to the Otherworld, Gran.' His legs ached as he wiped the sweat from his head.

She bit into her food and held up her wrinkled arm. 'I felt it too.' The large bracelet rolled down her skeletal wrist as she continued to chew on the sandwich. Small pictures illustrated both bracelets. The images on them changed regularly, shifting and moving in and out of sight. An aroma of strong coffee wafted around the room. The old woman pulled out her dentures and cackled spit across the room. 'Do you want anything to eat?' She placed her food on the table and stared at the young man. 'You look like you could do with fattening up; you've lost weight since I saw you last.'

He removed his jacket and held out his arm.

'I was here yesterday, Gran, and this is solid muscle.'

His physique was impressive enough to attract plenty of admiring glances when he went to the gym. Her eyes glazed over as she scrunched her face to peer at him.

'You're a good boy, Kylian; your parents would be proud of you.'

He shook his head and touched the bracelet on his wrist when it pulsated against his skin. It concerned and excited him at the same time.

Kylian pulled up a chair. 'We need to pack our bags.'

He'd never liked the smell of coffee and frowned at the pot on the table. Every day he visited her, he worried she'd have forgotten who he was, forgotten what their mission was. Tomato sauce dribbled down her chin as she spoke. The siren had spurred him into action, but she didn't appear to be in a hurry to answer its call.

'I'm not going with you, Kylian.'

With her wrinkled flesh and pointy teeth, she resembled a vampire as the red sauce dripped on to the floor. Kylian's eyes stretched up to her forehead.

'What? I can't do this on my own.' Despair oozed from his voice.

'Look at me, Kylian.' The old woman finished her food and held out her fingers. The skin was yellow and covered in creases. 'I'm eighty-two; what help would I be to you?' Her laugh rattled her teeth.

Kylian held her hands in his and examined those cloudy green eyes.

'You know how to use the book. I don't.'

'You've completed the training,' Grandmother Morrigan said. 'You've completed the simulations, read all the books and reports. This is what you've prepared for.' The old woman was frail, but her voice was firm. 'You've also handled the orphans that slipped through the barrier recently, and all with impressive skill. The wendigo you killed in Scotland took great bravery.'

Kylian tried not to think of his last mission. He may

have slain the beast, but two locals died in the chaos. Their screams continued to haunt him every night.

He puffed out his chest and pretended to be brave.

'They were strays. This is somebody using the forbidden book.' Just the thought of it back in the world sent a shiver down his spine. He couldn't deal with it on his own. 'Whoever has it can bring any creature they want here. Things much worse than what I've dealt with.'

She gave him her biggest smile. 'You're strong enough to handle anything, Kylian.'

'No pressure, then.'

He laughed without feeling happy. She poured herself another cup of coffee. He winced as the fumes drifted up to his nose.

'You're ready to do the job our family has waited centuries to complete. There is nothing beyond your capabilities. I have faith in you.'

She gripped his fingers with what little strength she had left. His emotions were a quivering cocktail of excitement and nervousness. She was right; he'd killed many of the creatures since receiving the bracelet. What was happening now surely couldn't be any worse than the group of werewolves he dealt with on the Yorkshire Moors last month.

'You trust me with this?'

He needed her reassurance. She got out of her chair and reached for the photo album behind her. Her legs wobbled a little as she grabbed it and placed it on the table.

'You haven't looked through this in a long time.'

His grandmother's voice trembled, but there was steel in her eyes. This wasn't the book Kylian expected to be talking about. She opened it to the first page. He peered at the sepia-toned photographs pasted into the yellowing pages.

'I don't need to see them. I remember what my parents look like.'

They'd been dead for five years, but he saw them in his mind every single day.

She took his hands again. Her warmth travelled into him.

'You have his physical strength and her intelligence. They were ready to do this, but since they were taken, it's become your responsibility, and they both believed you could do this, just as I do.'

Kylian shifted his gaze from her and towards the book. His mother and father smiled at him from the images: photographs snapped before he was born. He turned the page over, flicking through photos of his parents enjoying themselves at the beach to reach the ones of him as a baby. He had a bright smile and a chubby face.

'I couldn't protect them, but I can save everybody else.'

His self-doubt vanished as he gazed at the family he'd lost. Before he closed the book, he removed an image of them and slipped it into his pocket.

His grandma smiled at him. 'The fate of the world is in safe hands.'

'I need to prepare to leave, Gran. Got to organise my things from the flat and get the weapons.' She nodded. 'But how will I find the book?'

'The next time they use it, you'll know the location.' She pointed at his wrist. 'Your bracelet acts as a beacon linked to those ancient pages. It will be like a GPS on your phone.'

Surprised laughter burst from Kylian. 'You can't send text messages on the mobile I gave you, but you know what GPS is?'

She grinned at him, those weathered lips turning upwards to the wart below her nose.

'I may be ancient, but I'm not living in the past.'

They laughed together. He forced the seriousness of his task from his mind, but it couldn't last forever.

'And what do I do when I find the book and its keeper?'

He stood and walked to her as she used her arm to wipe bits of food from her face.

'You do whatever you need to do to keep this world safe.'

'Should I bring the book here?'

She shook her head. 'You must destroy it, Kylian. Let nothing and no one stand in your way. The fate of humanity rests with you. If it releases the Goddess, there will be no saving any of us from her wrath.'

'There's no pressure, then, Gran,' he repeated, kissed her on the cheek and saying goodbye.

The Goddess. He'd been told the stories about her countless times over the years, but did he believe she existed? It didn't matter. The book and its user were the most important things. He smiled at his grandmother, but in his heart, he wondered if he'd see her again.

The cats screeched at him as he left. He took his time getting back, observing the city and its residents as he considered what he was about to do, a multitude of thoughts running through his head. Would he have the strength to do what was necessary? Would he panic? He entered his home, his heart threatening to beat fast enough to charge a car battery. He sorted through the messages on his phone and switched on the TV. The news was full of freak weather stories and climate disasters from across the globe.

And it will only get worse.

Kylian sat down and waited for the stranger to use the book again.

HE WAS DOZING when the alarm went off, surprised to be sleeping in the afternoon. He put it down to stress as he studied the geographical reading on the bracelet. Somewhere in the northeast of England, but no specific place identified. It didn't matter, that would come soon enough. Now he had to book a flight from Dublin to Newcastle.

He grabbed his things as he checked the next flights on his phone. It was only as he was paying for the ticket that he understood he'd need to put the bracelet in his luggage. It would attract too much attention at airport security, with the figures shifting every few seconds.

He'd received it on his thirteenth birthday and hadn't taken it off in the subsequent five years. Kylian ran his fingers over the metal before taking the photo from his pocket. In the image, his mother wore the bracelet, her eyes sparkling while it glittered. He'd promised never to remove it since that day, but now he had no choice.

Kylian slipped it off, a sense of dread invading him as he placed it in the bag. The book would need to be used again for him to get a precise hit in the northeast, but it would be. From what he'd learnt about it, he knew once someone activated it, they'd find it impossible to stop using it.

'It's an addiction,' his grandmother had told him.

Kylian locked the door behind him.

And like all addicts, they'll destroy everything around them to keep doing it.

9 THE CARNIVAL

Ella had a restless night, her thoughts consumed by what had happened to Dotty and her own part in her cousin's condition. Guilt continued to sweep through her when she went into the house to see the others. Aunt Ida was the only one there. She placed scrambled eggs on the table in front of Ella.

'No chores today. Your Uncle George is at the hospital with the girls.' Ida had huge black bags under her eyes as if she'd been up all night.

Ella stared at the food going cold. She should have been hungry, but there was an emptiness in her stomach which food couldn't fill.

'How is Dotty?'

'It's too early to say, but the doctors don't think she'll get better.'

She expected tears from Ida, but there was nothing. Ella had to control hers as she placed her hands below the table to hide the shaking.

'What happened?'

Ida cradled a cup of hot coffee in her fingers.

'There was a fight at school. Dotty was knocked to the ground and banged her head. You weren't there?'

Ella had never been a good liar, but she had to be now.

'No. I left with my friends as soon as the bell went.'

The hairs on her arms stood on end as she peered into Ida's eyes. For the first time since she'd arrived in the Twist house, she saw something of her mother in her aunt.

'That's what Dolly said. Thank God you weren't involved.'

The sympathy in her voice shocked Ella. The family had given her nothing but grief since arriving, but all she felt now was sadness for them. And Dolly had lied for her.

'Who was fighting?'

Somebody must have mentioned seeing the knocker. The shaking moved from her fingers and along her arms.

'It was some child from another school. I guess it was an accident.' Ida got up. 'But you make sure you stay safe today.'

Her concern appeared genuine, and Ella didn't know what to think. She was worried about Dotty in the hospital, but she also remembered what Dolly had said to her last night, recalling the threats her cousin had made.

'I will, Aunt Ida.'

She waited for the trembling to stop. She finished her breakfast, washed the dishes and went to school. She'd left Ratter in the barn, but she carried the book with her. Ella wouldn't use it again, but wanted nobody to find it by accident under the bed.

When she arrived at school, all the talk was about the fight. A bunch of kids claimed a big, ugly teenager from the next village had started it. Some younger ones thought it was a monster; others said it was an attraction from the carnival which had got loose and run wild. That became the most popular rumour as children whispered about visiting the carnival.

'We should go after school.' Billy sat next to Ella in class. 'Take our minds off what happened to your cousin.'

'I must visit the hospital.' It was the only thought in her head.

'Is the kid in a coma?' Dora joined them. Ella nodded.

'Eyes to the front, children.'

Miss Barkay got the registration underway. The rest of the day flew by in a blur, with Ella unable to pay attention to anything. By the end of lesson five, Billy had convinced her to go to the carnival.

'How far is this racecourse?' Dora said as they exited the school gates. Ella expected to feel Dolly's hands on her shoulder any second.

'About an hour's walk,' she replied. 'Ten minutes by train.'

Dora grinned. 'Train it is, then.'

Ella turned out her empty pockets. 'I can't go.'

Billy pulled at his trousers. 'It's all right; I'll pay. I got me pocket money today.'

The station was small, but was one of the oldest in the world. There was a train ready to depart when they got there. They scrambled on board as the conductor put a whistle to his mouth. Billy never stopped talking all the way there, yacking about his football, his comics, his computer games. It helped Ella to relax and she was grateful for it.

Dora was quiet, staring out of the window at the sea. Some other kids from school were at the back of the carriage. Ella hoped they'd leave her alone without Dolly there to guide them. She pushed the guilt about Dotty to the side as the train arrived at their destination. The three of them jumped off and dashed towards the racecourse.

'Last one there buys the candy floss,' Billy shouted as he raced ahead.

'What's candy floss?' Dora ran next to Ella.

'Sugar delight,' Ella replied with a smile on her face.

Thoughts of hospitals and dangerous Elementals she'd let loose in the world slipped to the back of her mind. The two girls picked up their pace, going past Billy and reaching the gate first. Ella had her ticket in her eager outstretched hand.

'Looks like the sweets are on you, Billy Pudding.' Ella laughed as he followed in behind them.

His scowl was as dark as the clouds gathering above.

'It's my fault for faffing about.'

He pushed his hands into his pockets in search of money. Ella skipped her way into the carnival. It was still early, so the crowds hadn't gathered yet.

'I've never been to a carnival.' Dora caught up with her. They grinned at each other as if they'd been friends for life.

'My parents took me to a circus a few years ago, but I didn't like it.' Ella stood in front of the dodgems. Having to watch the animals performing tricks had upset her so much, she'd refused to eat anything when they got home. 'I hope this will be more interesting.'

She scanned the surroundings. All she saw were things you'd get at a regular funfair, rides and attractions, and no sign of the promised curiosities and marvels. She sighed when two men dressed as cats walked towards her. Following them was a woman looking like a medieval Queen sitting on a horse with a horn attached to its head.

Billy arrived with the candy floss. 'That's a terrible looking unicorn.'

Ella grabbed hers, taking a chunk from it as she dodged the human felines and their attempt at getting her attention. When she came up for air, pink floss clung to her cheeks like a colourful cloud. Somebody dressed as Superman ran past them, making strange whooshing noises.

'This is a waste of time.' Ella swept dry sugar from her face, unable to hide her disappointment.

'They must keep the good stuff from the public.' Billy spoke as he chewed on the candy floss. 'Especially the spider baby.'

'What?' Ella licked the stick clean.

'The spider baby,' Billy repeated. 'It has the body of a spider and the head of a baby.' He smirked as he smacked his lips.

'Don't be silly,' Ella scoffed at him.

'He's not wrong.' Dora slurped down her candy floss. 'Give me the book, and I'll show you.'

Ella stared at Dora. She'd told herself she wouldn't use the book until the guide promised by the Elemental arrived. But surely it couldn't hurt to look at it? And if Dora was holding it, then Ella's thoughts couldn't cause problems. She handed it to her, glad to have the responsibility somewhere else.

Dora turned it over and pointed to the third row down and the illustration in the middle.

'Does that seem familiar?'

Ella and Billy peered at what looked like an insect with a human head.

'It's the spider baby,' Billy shouted as Ella shivered.

'What is it?' Ella asked Dora.

'It's called a ghast. It's the offspring of a banshee and a human. To be avoided whenever possible.'

Ella stared at Dora, amazed again at how much knowledge she had. A sudden idea came to her.

What if Dora is the person sent to teach me how to use the book?

Billy grimaced. 'I don't want to see one of those up close.'

'They're supposed to have sharp teeth and stink worse than rotting garbage.'

Dora appeared excited by the thought, but Billy shivered.

'It sounds like a reet manky codger.'

'There are many friendly Elementals as well,' Dora said as they strode past the Big Wheel and the screaming kids on top of it. 'If you want to see a real unicorn, it's two rows above the ghast.' She returned the book to Ella.

'I'm scared to do it again.'

Ella took the book between her shaking fingers. She didn't want the others seeing what was wrong with her. Dora placed her hand on Ella's.

'What happened with your cousin was an accident. You must get the hang of this.'

Ella hesitated, but she so wanted to see a unicorn. And if she willed it here, people would only think it was part of the carnival. Her doubts vanished as Dora smiled at her. Billy jigged around them as Irish dance music burst out of invisible speakers above their heads. The place was warming up.

She pressed her finger into the illustration, her mind conjuring up images of sitting on the unicorn and riding along the beach. When nothing had happened after two minutes, her shoulders slumped, and she gave up.

'I don't think I'm any good at this.' She handed the book to Dora.

'Are you sure?'

The other girl pointed to the air shimmering in front of

them. This differed from when the knocker appeared. The horn came first, gleaming in the sun as it pushed its way into the world, then the head, followed by the rest. It was a magnificent sight.

Ella wiped a tear from her eye as she stepped towards the unicorn.

'We all have to hug it.'

Billy stopped dancing. 'What?'

'The Elemental in the house told me the nice ones need our love.' She forgot her reservations about using the book and threw her arms around the unicorn's neck. The connection between them was immediate, a heat passing from her and into the magical creature. All of Ella's doubts about what had happened to Dotty disappeared. There was joy in her which hadn't been there since the disappearance of her parents. All the pain of her recent life vanished. 'C'mon, Billy, Dora, grab hold.' There was a delight in her voice and happiness in her heart. Billy appeared reluctant at first, but Ella's smile convinced him. He inched closer to her and placed one hand on the unicorn's back.

'It's... it's... magical,' he stuttered. Ella took his hand and beamed at him.

'Join us, Dora,' Ella said. The other girl hesitated, and Ella guessed she was afraid.

Dora stood back. 'You need to bring a pixie over.'

'What?' Ella replied.

'Unicorns and pixies have a unique connection.'

Ella didn't question the idea, convinced now Dora was the one to show her the correct way to use the book. She let go of the unicorn and removed the book from her pocket, scanning the front until she found the image she wanted halfway down. She touched the picture and imagined the creature joining them.

'Ow.' Something landed on Ella's shoulder. She thought it was a bird, turning to stare at it and gazing straight into the sparkling eyes of the pixie. 'Oh my.' The creature's blue skin shimmered under the sun as its wings flickered against Ella's hair and its pointed ears tickled her chin. She pushed the book into her trousers and held out a hand for the small Elemental. It jumped into her palm and she laughed. This was beyond her wildest dreams. Its tiny feet delighted her flesh, its eyes twinkling at her as she moved towards the unicorn.

A fantastic idea became fully formed in her head.

'I could do this to find my parents.'

The pixie pirouetted in her hand. Ella had a connection with the creature which felt euphoric. She guessed it was the Light travelling between them.

'What do ya mean?' Billy scrunched his face at her.

'I can use the book to bring them here.' Before Dora and Billy said anything, Ella pictured it in her brain. 'Come here, Mum and Dad, come to me now.'

She said the words as the pixie stroked her palm with its tiny delicate fingers. Her mind was so full of wonder, she didn't hear Billy shouting. The fist hit the side of her head like a comet crashing to earth. The pixie and the book tumbled from Ella's hand in slow motion as she fell to the ground with a wallop.

Thunder vibrated inside Ella's head. Her legs trembled as the pixie floated near the long grass. Daisy stretched out and kicked the tiny creature towards her sister.

'I told ya she's the Devil's kid.' Daisy's voice grated against Ella's one good ear.

'Whatever she is, she'll pay for what she did to Dotty.' Dolly grabbed the book and placed her big foot over the squirming pixie. 'I'll squash this thing, and then we'll deal with her.'

'What about this fake unicarn?' Daisy said as the unicorn moved towards the Twist sisters. It seemed uninterested in what was going on around it.

'Ignore it.' Dolly lowered her shoe on to the squealing pixie.

Ella crawled on the grass and peered at her cousins.

'Don't.' Dora stepped forward. 'We can save your sister.'

'What?' Dolly's mouth dropped open.

'Ella can save Dotty.' Dora inched towards Dolly's hovering leg. Ella picked herself up, looking as bemused as her relatives. 'If you kill the pixie, your sister will stay in a coma for the rest of her life.'

Dora knelt and put her head at risk from the oldest Twist. Dolly wavered for a second before lowering her foot from the trembling Elemental. Dora scooped the pixie up and stood next to Ella.

Dolly clenched her fists. 'You've got a minute to explain this madness.'

Ella pushed aside her fear and found the courage to stand up to her cousin. She placed one hand on the unicorn and its strength flowed through her. It was like being plugged into an electrical socket, but instead of the power hurting her, it invigorated Ella. Somehow, she thought, the Elemental had taken the Light Ella had given it only a few minutes ago and then transformed it into something extraordinary. And then the unicorn had passed it back to Ella. She'd read about something like this in her biology class: her teachers called it symbiosis. The whole of Ella's body vibrated, but this wasn't like the shakes she'd got before; this was as if she was bursting with positivity.

She stood up straight with her chest out and stared into Dolly's eyes.

'Give me the book and I'll bring Dotty out of her coma.'

She didn't know how she'd do it, but Dora's words and the look on her face told her there must be an Elemental that could help. The Light from the unicorn made her feel as if she could do anything.

Dolly growled as she held on to the book. 'Explain this nonsense first.'

Ella glared back at her. 'I can bring magical creatures out of that, and I'll find something to save Dotty.'

She couldn't be bothered to explain Elementals and how they came from another dimension parallel to this one.

She didn't understand how it worked, so how could her cousins?

Daisy stared at the pixie in Dora's palm. 'Told ya she's Devil's spawn.'

Dolly ignored her sister and opened the book, peering at the unicorn images and the pixie. She appeared unfazed by what was going on around her, totally focused on her young cousin.

She threw the book at Ella, who caught it in one hand.

'Let's go to the hospital now. And bring the unicorn.' She grabbed Billy by the collar and dragged him to her. 'You're coming as well, Pudding. I'll crush your head if this doesn't work.'

He grimaced, and Ella was afraid for him. Dolly pushed him in front of her as she headed for the exit. The crowds were just arriving as they left, gazing at the unicorn in stunned silence.

'I hope this works,' Ella whispered to Dora as they followed.

It was a twenty-minute walk to the hospital, five kids, a pixie and a unicorn marching through the town. People stared and gasped as they strode by. Some brave souls approached them and stroked the horned creature. Ella thought about shouting at them until she remembered the Elemental wanted this type of contact. She imagined the Light travelling from human to Elemental and vice versa, and she considered what she was about to do in the hospital. She didn't think twice about those taking photos and recording on their phones.

'Family only,' Dolly said to them when they got there. 'But Daisy will stay here and monitor you two.' She pointed at Billy and Dora before striding towards the entrance.

Ella grabbed Dora's free hand. 'What should I do?'

Dora whispered into Ella's ear. 'Choose the most powerful Elemental you see on the cover. They'll do the rest.'

Ella rushed into the building, all her reservations about using the book having evaporated inside the carnival.

'Dotty's in a private room.'

Dolly pushed the door to the stairs open. They walked up together in silence. When they reached the second floor, Dolly took Ella past a reception desk and a group of nurses who gave the two of them grim smiles. Dolly went first and they stepped inside. The place was sparse and white apart from the fresh flowers someone had brought. The smell of nature was in stark contrast to the rest of the room.

Ella clutched her chest when she stared at Dotty. 'Oh, my!'

Dotty gazed into space, every part of her face frozen as shadows consumed the flesh under her eyes.

Dolly glared at Ella. 'If what you said is true about bringing creatures out of the book, then you're responsible for this with that giant who attacked us yesterday.'

Ella pressed the book into her chest. 'I'm sorry.'

'It's time to keep your promise.'

Dolly held on to her younger sister's hand and wiped a tear from her face. It shocked Ella to witness such a show of emotion from her cousin. She forgot why she was there until Dora's words came back to her.

Choose the most powerful Elemental you see on the cover. They'll do the rest.

Ella scrutinised both sides of the book deciding on the most potent Elemental. She knew as soon as she saw it, pressing her finger into the front as Dolly scowled at her. Her skills were improving every time she used the book, and the Elemental appeared immediately.

'Jesus!' Dolly gawked at the woman in the black suit.

'Not quite,' the witch said. 'But I met him once.' Ella's face froze as she stared at the Elemental with the long dark hair. She wasn't expecting a witch to look like this. It was as if she'd stepped out of a business meeting. 'Do either of you have a fag?' The witch smiled at them. 'It's so long since I've had a smoke.' Ella and Dolly were too stunned to respond. 'You must be the keeper of the book.' She moved towards Ella and held out her hand. 'My name is Seraphina.'

Ella defrosted her limbs and found the energy to shake that hand. It was like ice to the touch and she flinched at it.

'Yes, it's much colder where I come from, but you get used to it. And you are?' The witch's eyes were different colours, one brown and one blue. They mesmerised Ella.

'I'm... I'm... I'm....' Ella couldn't get the rest of the words out.

'She's Ella, I'm Dolly, and you're here to help my sister, Dotty.' Dolly had regained her confidence in this strange situation.

Seraphina turned to face her. 'Is that so, sugar lump?' She glanced at Ella. 'Is this true, bookkeeper?' Seraphina smiled, and a shiver shot down Ella's spine.

'Ye-es,' Ella stuttered.

'Well, dear bookkeeper, I'm not one of the lower-level creatures. I do nothing unless I want to, and I'd need something in return.'

The witch went to the bed and stared into Dotty's face.

'What do you want?' Dolly's voice was full of menace.

Seraphina ignored her and turned to Ella. 'Does sugar lump speak for you?'

'Can you help her?' Ella pointed at Dotty.

The Elemental arched her eyebrows and laughed.

'I wouldn't be much of a witch if I couldn't, would I?'

Dolly moved to the bed and took hold of her sister's hand.

'You'll do it, or I'll hurt both of you.'

The witch slipped into a seat and filed her fingernails.

'I need to look my best if I'll be living amongst humans again, which is why I chose these modern clothes. And they're much more comfortable than those long dresses I used to wear.' She whistled as she worked at her nails.

Ella gripped the book until her fingers ached.

'What do you want in exchange?'

Seraphina didn't look up from her manicure.

'You must promise not to send me back to the other side.'

Ella took a deep breath. 'Why stay here?'

Seraphina twisted her head and turned up her nose. She'd stopped filing her nails and was busy applying purple polish to them with an invisible brush.

'Don't you want to live here?'

'Yes, of course I do.'

'Then why wouldn't I?' Amusement covered Seraphina's face. 'It's very dull on the other side, you know. The place is all grey and miserable with nobody interesting to talk to. This world is much more fun.'

The room stank of varnish and Ella scrunched her nose at the smell.

'Don't you speak to the other witches?'

Seraphina pursed her lips and shook her head.

'Oh no, there's nothing like that over there. We all dislike each other very much. Some of them are such awful creatures. You were lucky it was me who answered your call.'

'You're a good witch?'

Seraphina grinned. 'Of course I am, silly.' Her laugh

echoed around the room like a lullaby. 'If I'd been a bad witch, I'd have eaten you both and taken the book for myself.' Ella trembled as her legs turned to jelly. 'I'll tell you some secrets about it if that will help convince you.'

Seraphina made herself at home, rummaging through the small chest of drawers near the bed.

'Okay.' Ella was struggling with what to do.

Dolly stared at them like a dog irritated by a postal worker.

'You better do this soon.'

'Don't worry, sugar lump; you'll get your sister back. I need to explain something to the bookkeeper first.' She peered deep into Ella's eyes. 'The book you hold is thousands of years old. Nobody knows who created it, but only certain people can use it. Magic was used to banish all Elementals from the earthly plane. This was completed over centuries, and the book works as a connection between the two worlds. Think of it as a doorway and its user as the key. The book accesses the great natural barrier formed to keep the likes of me on the other side, but man's tampering with nature has weakened it in spots, so every once in a while an Elemental will stumble through.'

Ella peered at the witch. 'Wouldn't we see them when they do?'

'Sometimes you do, but you dismiss them as your imagination or a hallucination. Some Elementals can possess living things, so they're here, but you aren't aware of it. That connection is hazardous over time, though, to both the host and the Elemental.'

The witch's words fascinated Ella. 'What happens then?'

'Nothing good.' Seraphina frowned.

'If we continue to damage nature and the environment, what will happen?'

'Nothing good,' Seraphina replied.

'Enough of this chattering,' Dolly shouted. 'Save my sister.'

Ella stared at her cousins, and then at the witch. There was only one choice she could make.

'I promise not to send you back if you can help Dotty.'

Seraphina smiled like a lizard licking its lips.

'You made a wise decision, bookkeeper.' She lifted from the ground, floated over the bed to the other side. Ella gasped as Seraphina placed her hands on Dotty's forehead. 'How I've missed this world.'

The witch caressed the head of the girl in the coma.

11 THE UNICORN, THE WITCH AND
THE HOSPITAL

'You better not hurt her,' Dolly growled at the witch. As much as Ella disliked her oldest cousin, she admired her fierce determination in the face of the strangeness which had entered her world.

'This child has nothing to fear from me.' Seraphina's fingers appeared to blend into Dotty's flesh, and the witch's actions transfixed Ella. 'Because I've been away from this planet for so long, my full powers are returning slowly. But I still have enough juice to return your sister to her true self.' She peered at Ella with a mischievous smile. 'I'm not sure it would be a good thing for you, though.' Seraphina's hands disappeared up to the knuckles inside Dotty's forehead.

Confusion crawled across Ella's face.

'Why?'

She stared at the bizarre scene and flinched a little. It was as if Seraphina and Dotty were joined like strange Siamese twins.

'Dark thoughts possess this girl, some too terrible to describe, and most of them are about you, Ella Finn. Are you sure you want me to continue?'

Dolly glared at Ella while Seraphina kept her shimmering fingers inside Dotty's skull.

'Of course.'

It didn't matter how much Dotty hated her. It was Ella's fault she was in the hospital, and she'd do anything to get her back. Even make a pact with a witch she wasn't sure she trusted.

Seraphina concentrated on the patient for two more minutes before untangling her flesh from the stricken girl. A whoosh swirled through the air, and for some unknown reason, the room stank of pickled onions. It made Ella feel hungry and sick at the same time.

'There, she's as good as new.' Seraphina stepped from the bed and moved towards the window. 'Though perhaps good is not the right description.'

Dotty lay as if nothing had changed. Steam came out of Dolly's nose and a low rumbling noise drifted from her throat as she clenched her fists and glared at the witch. Then Dotty sat up with a start and spewed all over the room.

Ella moved back against the wall to avoid the vomit.

'Damn!'

Seraphina rested one hand on the glass.

'That bit is never pleasant for anyone.'

Dolly grabbed her sister in a bear hug as the younger Twist coughed louder than an exploding volcano. A heavy weight lifted from Ella's mind.

Maybe everything will be all right now.

'How did you do that?'

She approached the witch. The place reeked of fresh puke and Ella wanted the pickled onions to return. Seraphina kept her back to her as she spoke.

'How much do you know about the book in your possession?'

'Not a lot.' Ella saw no point in lying. 'Someone is coming to teach me how to use it.'

'Is that so?' Seraphina turned to face her, her unusual eyes glittering like tiny disco balls. Her flesh was smooth and flawless. 'And who might that lucky person be?' She peered deep into Ella like a worm burrowing under her skin. Ella winced.

'I don't know, but they're coming from far away.' She found steel at the bottom of her gut. 'And they'll show me how to save the world.'

'Well, you better learn how to use it soon, because the barrier between worlds weakens every time your kind pollutes the planet. If the holes get big enough, then the angriest Elementals will come through, and you won't want to be around for that.'

Dolly and Dotty were crying behind them, and Ella didn't know what was stranger: the witch's words or her cousins' tears.

'What type of Elemental do you mean?'

She ignored the Twist sisters and stared at the witch. Seraphina's smile was both cruel and intoxicating.

'Gods and monsters, child.' Seraphina's teeth were a brilliant white. 'There will be gods and monsters, and your world will never be the same.' The chill in her voice sent ice into Ella's heart. 'Speaking of which, is that your unicorn attracting a large crowd outside?'

'Crap.'

Ella ran to the window. In the hospital car park, a group of people surrounded the horned Elemental, and she couldn't see Billy and Dora anywhere.

'The human authorities will be here soon. If they don't

kill the unicorn, they'll lock it up. It is the way of all men to cage the things they don't understand. What will you do then?'

'I don't know.'

Fear replaced the relief from Dotty's recovery. She didn't want to send the unicorn back, but there was no telling what those people were doing to it down there.

A faint transient smile slipped across Seraphina's face. 'I can help you.'

Ella hesitated, staring at her cousins as they whispered to each other. Dotty wiped sick from her lips. Seraphina's smirk made Ella uneasy.

'Why would you do that?' She suspected the witch's motives.

'A favour for a favour, from me to you, and then back again.'

Seraphina strode to the door.

'What do you want?'

Ella was concentrating on the growing chaos outside. People were hanging all over the unicorn. Her heart ached with what they were doing to it.

'I want nothing now. But in the future, I'll come to you and ask for a favour.'

Ella didn't know what to do. She shouldn't trust the witch, even after what she'd done for Dotty. The screams outside the window convinced her she only had one choice.

'Yes, I agree.' Ella spoke with urgency. 'I promise to give a favour for a favour.'

'You'll do whatever I ask?'

'Yes.'

Ella's fears for her cousin had transferred to the unicorn. The shouts grew louder as the crowd increased.

She pressed her head against the window, wishing she could see where Dora and Billy were.

'Then follow me, bookkeeper, before the mob starts selling bits of the creature as lucky charms.'

Seraphina left the room and Ella ran after her. Her feet bounced off the steps as they headed downstairs, Seraphina floating a few inches above the ground as they moved. Confusion reigned at the entrance as medical staff ignored their duties and clamoured to see what was happening outside. The chaos frightened Ella.

'What are you going to do?'

'I could make all these humans disappear.'

Seraphina pushed through them and out of the building. Ella was shocked at the idea of it.

'You mean, kill them?'

She stumbled towards the growing crowd. Was Seraphina a bad witch after all?

'Don't be silly.' Seraphina stood beside her. 'I'll only send them to another place, just like their ancestors did to me and my kind centuries ago.' Ella detected the bitterness in her voice. 'Maybe to the moon or one of those planets humans are always desperate to get to.' They stopped at the edge of the crowd. The unicorn's horn was visible over the top of the mass of people, but she still couldn't see either Billy or Dora. Dozens of hands grasped at the horn, and Ella feared someone would try to tear it from the animal's head. They had to do something quickly, but the witch appeared unconcerned by the urgency in Ella's face.

'Do you think men want to travel to other worlds so they can ruin them as they've done this one, destroy the land and the sea and the air in the pursuit of greed and meaningless material wealth?'

Ella didn't know what to say, searching for her friends

instead. The mob became more frenzied as some of them took selfies with the unicorn. A teenage boy tried to climb on to the animal, but a familiar figure dragged him off.

'Pack it in,' the ginger-haired gap-toothed kid shouted at the much older and much bigger boy. Billy pushed him into the crowd as the kid glared at him.

'Billy!' Ella ran towards him. He turned from the mob and hugged her. For Ella, it seemed the most natural thing in the world.

They separated as Seraphina gazed into the sky.

The witch let out a giant sigh.

'Ahhhhh, to feel nature on my face again is a wonderful thing.' She stared into the clouds, and then the surrounding crowd. 'To be denied the comforts of your birth is both cruel and capricious. It would serve these people right if I sent them all into the other realm.'

Billy ignored her and spoke to Ella.

'I'm jiggered trying to keep everyone away.' Sweat dripped from his face. He bent over to catch his breath before straightening his back. 'We were waiting in the shadows when some patients spotted us and approached the unicorn. And then more and more appeared and everyone wanted to stroke her.'

The words sputtered from him, his voice on the edge of tears, his arms trembling like branches in the wind. Ella squeezed his fingers and smiled at him.

'It's okay now. This is Seraphina, and she's going to help us. Where's Dora?'

Billy eyed the witch suspiciously. He shook his head and wiped his lips with the top of his arm.

'I don't know,' he stuttered. 'I lost track of her when all these people appeared. I think she might be narked off at sommat.'

Seraphina waved her hand in the air.

'They'll suck the life from her soon.'

'How?' Ella held on to Billy's hand.

'Do you know about Light?'

'A little.'

'It's what we're all made of, both humans and Elementals, at a micro-level. At different stages of our existence, it flows between both species; with one sustaining the other. When the Goddess created all life, She intended for us to live together in symbiosis. Do you know what that is?'

Ella gazed at the witch. 'I've just been thinking about the same thing.'

Billy shook his head 'What is it?'

Seraphina dismissed him with a flick of her eyelids.

'It doesn't matter now, but centuries ago, men corrupted the world and tricked the Goddess into banishing all Elementals into the other realm.' Sadness dripped from her every word. 'Men believed they didn't need the Light to exist, that they didn't need it to find meaning in existence. All they wanted was power and wealth, pursuing pleasure regardless of the consequences.' She paused, and Ella feared she wouldn't help them. 'It's so long since these humans have encountered a creature as magnificent as a unicorn, they'll overdose on its Light.'

Ella clasped at her throat. 'Do something.'

Patients, relatives and random bystanders were drawn to the unicorn like walking shards of metal dragged towards a magnet. Happiness convulsed their faces as they stroked the four-legged wonder. Ella was wide-eyed, amazed it hadn't kicked its way out of the crowd.

'Unicorns are passive creatures,' Seraphina said as if reading Ella's mind.

'Can you save it?' Ella pleaded.

'I promised I would, and I will. Since I can't remove these troublesome humans, where would you like to go?'

It was a simple question for Ella to answer and test Seraphina's abilities simultaneously.

'There's a secret house on the clifftops that only I can see. Will you take us there?'

Seraphina was going to move people out of the way, but froze at Ella's words.

'You have the book and you can enter the gateway? I may have misjudged you, child.' Her eyes filled with surprise. 'Take hold of my hand.'

Ella did that as Seraphina forced her way through the crowd, and they laid their fingers on the unicorn. Ella held on to Billy as a surge of energy rushed through her. She imagined this was what it would feel like to be struck by lightning.

She was about to say something when they all disappeared as dozens of people caught the event on their phones.

12 THE PRIORY

Vanishing from one place and then reappearing in another was a strange sensation. Ella's guts churned like jelly in a microwave and something dry gripped the back of her throat. There were bright lights everywhere, but she stared through the illumination and gazed at her hands. The stink of gasoline made her nose wince.

I'm not shaking.

She didn't have time to appreciate what that meant before a horn screamed in her ears. Ella peered through the light as the ten-tonne truck hurtled towards her. She stood in the middle of a motorway as death raced forward. Ella clutched at her chest and gasped for breath.

The sickness overcame her once more as she disappeared again. It was dark when she landed, her feet sloshing through swamp water and mud. She breathed slowly, her hands touching leaves and branches either side of her. An aroma of Palma violets lingered in the air as oppressive heat settled over Ella's body. Pinpricks of light blinked in the gloom.

She took two seconds to realise the lights were eyes staring at her: inhuman eyes.

'Ella, are you there?'

Billy's voice cut through the murk. She felt better for hearing him.

'I can't see you, Billy.'

The animal eyes were like a cluster of stars in the night sky. And some of them were getting closer to her.

'Where are we?' His fear was clear to her.

'I don't know, but we're not alone.'

Anger gripped her heart, irritation at her stupidity for trusting the witch. Billy was silent as low rumbling growls accompanied those animal eyes. Insects fluttered around her face and she tried to swat them away. Her legs inched backwards through the mud. The heat was unbearable, sweeping down on her like a blanket created from the sun.

'I can see you, Ella. I'm on your left.'

Moonlight burst through the trees, and she followed his voice to the side. He sat in a tree like Tarzan and she grinned at the sight. She'd be safe up there if she could climb quickly enough.

Before she could do anything, something pounced on her. She fell backwards, pinned to the ground by something little and hairy. Ella's reflexes kicked in, her hand reaching up and grabbing fur and flesh between her fingers. Whatever the animal was, it was small and she threw it off her.

Some of its companions crept towards her as an aroma of wet fuzz and fiery breath washed over Ella's face. She wanted to gag as the pinpricks of light grew into balls of fire and jumped at her.

Billy yelled as Ella vanished again.

Water was gushing down her throat when she reappeared. Seawater flowed into her nose, her ears, and stopped her from screaming. Gravity pulled at her legs as she sank further beneath the waves. Something large and scaly brushed past her as Ella struggled against the damp weight forcing her further and further underwater. She tried to breathe, arms grappling at the liquid engulfing her. Her lungs filled as her mind drifted. She descended into the abyss as everything went dark and the cold cut through her skin and into her bones. Ella shook in the wet gloom as tiny fish nibbled at her fingers before she disappeared again.

She hit dry ground and spluttered water from her mouth, expecting her lungs and heart to spill everywhere. Her chest had a liquid lead weight on it, forcing choking spasms through her upper body. She was still shivering and possessed by bitter ice when somebody got hold of her and slapped her back.

'Spit it all out.'

Billy held on to her with one arm while whacking her spine with the other. Ella kept on coughing, ignoring the dampness and agony before sprawling on to the ground. She peered into a perfect blue sky dotted with marshmallow clouds. Perhaps she'd drowned and this was the vision of the next life.

He leant over and pushed wet hair from Ella's eyes. 'Are you okay?'

'I think so.'

The back of her throat throbbed. She imagined a fish wriggling inside her mouth, forcing her to push Billy out of the way and spew saltwater all over the grass. She coughed up bits of seaweed and felt like crap.

'I'm sorry, children; I'm not at my best yet.' Seraphina sat opposite them, cigarette in hand, smoke billowing from her mouth. 'But at least I picked up a packet of fags from the shops outside.' The witch seemed unconcerned by Ella's anguish.

Ella ignored the pain flowing through her and pulled her body up. Ruins of old buildings and the wild countryside surrounded them. Her fingers shook with anger, and she had to stop herself from rushing at the witch and choking the life from her.

'How come I was the only one who ended up underwater?' The heat in her veins dried her skin.

Seraphina blew smoke towards her.

'A temporary glitch in the space-time continuum.'

Ella glared at her, unsure if she was playing games at her expense.

Billy slumped to the ground. 'I'm knackered.'

'How easy do you think it is to move bodies across the layers of space? And neither of you is the lightest, I have to say. What you children eat in this modern world is staggeringly unhealthy.' Seraphina appeared to have found something else to rant about. 'All this sugar and junk food you consume is terrible. Stick to a nice piece of fruit and the occasional carrot, and you'll be miles healthier, I promise you.'

'You sound like my mother,' Billy said.

Seraphina pouted at his words.

'I assume she's a most sensible adult doing all she can to look after her ungrateful child.'

'This isn't the cliffs.'

Ella squeezed the water from her trousers, but she was still sodden. Her chest ached and her throat felt as if it had shrunk to half its size and someone had stuffed an overcooked jacket potato inside it.

'Let me help you with that.' Seraphina waved her hand at Ella. She appeared to have forgotten her rant at Billy, and

Ella's damp clothes were dry instantly. The witch finished her cigarette with a flourish, blowing out smoke resembling a dragon soaring into the clouds. She was about to drop the stub on to the ground, but flicked it at Billy instead. He flinched as it disappeared into nothing.

'I'm still getting my bearings with transportation, so I thought we might have a rest before heading to the gateway between worlds.' Seraphina peered around their surroundings. 'I didn't expect it to be this dilapidated; it was so beautiful the last time I was here.' There was a reflective tone to her voice.

Ella relaxed into her now warm and dry clothes, staring at the surrounding ruins. A magnificent archway stood on its own at the other end from them, flanked by rows of trees where buildings would have been. Dotted around the overgrown grass were scattered architectural skeletons.

There was peacefulness to the area which put Ella at ease.

'What is this place?'

Billy laid his arm on her shoulder and she was glad he was with her.

'This is Gisborough Priory. My dad brought me here a few times. It's only a few miles from the coast.'

Ella grabbed at her throat, remembering her recent jaunt underwater. Even though she was keen to get back to the mystery house, she was in no rush to see the sea again soon.

'Some monks here were naughty boys.' Seraphina grinned at them. 'They were not very devout at all.'

Ella ran her fingers through the moss on the stones, putting behind her those dangerous fleeting visits on the road, in the jungle and under the ocean. She surprised herself with how strong she was becoming. Ella spat the last of the seawater from her bruised throat, sighing heavily as energy returned to her.

She looked up to see the unicorn chewing on the grass.

'You've been here before?'

She still viewed the witch with distrust, wondering if Seraphina had created those dangerous jumps deliberately.

Maybe she's trying to scare me because she wants the book to herself.

'It was a long time ago. The priory's residents and I had something important in common.'

Another cigarette magically appeared in Seraphina's hand. She lit it with a flick of her purple nails.

'And what was that?' Ella asked.

The more she learnt about the witch, the better she'd understand her. And perhaps she could work out what favour Seraphina would eventually demand of her.

'We were both persecuted by the King and his sycophants.' A nostalgic look crossed Seraphina's face as she stared at the children. She turned her eyes from them and gazed into the ground. 'At least the passageway is still here.'

Billy gawked at her in confusion. 'There's nothing left but ruins.'

'My original spell of deception still works after all this time.'

Seraphina beamed at them as they waited for an explanation. Ella had lost her urgency to return to the mystery house, allowing herself to relax in the surroundings. Plus, she didn't want to risk travelling through one of the witch's transportation spells again.

She ran a finger through her damp hair.

'What's a spell of deception?'

Perhaps Seraphina had cast such a thing over her in the hospital, and this was all a trick.

'To thank the monks for giving me a safe place to stay, I helped them create an underground passage leading from the priory when the dissolution came. At the other end is a cave under the hills in which a raven stands guard over a chest of gold.'

Billy's eyes lit up at her words and Ella didn't know what to think. One second she viewed Seraphina with suspicion, the next she was overjoyed with this magical new world she'd fallen in to.

'Is the gold still there?' Billy said.

Seraphina wagged her finger at him.

'If you can discover the passageway and answer the raven's questions, you could find out for yourself.'

Ella warmed to the witch. 'What happened to you, Seraphina?'

'Well, that's a long story for another day but let's say I had an unfortunate run-in with the Witchfinder General.'

Ella had read the history of the witch trials in England and the ill-fated hanged women, but she never thought she'd get the chance to speak to a real live one.

'Do you talk to the Devil?'

Billy's question surprised even Ella. Seraphina let out a high-pitched laugh which scattered the birds loitering in the trees.

'There's no such thing as the Devil, silly boy.' Seraphina shook her head at him. 'Evil exists, but it comes from there.' She pointed at his heart and he grimaced.

'Are you the person sent to show me how to use this?'

Ella gripped the book, scanning the cover, but with one eye on Seraphina. The witch lifted from the ground and floated towards her. Billy gasped and Ella marvelled at the sight.

'You don't need me or anybody else to show you what to

do, Ella Finn. All you require is to believe in yourself. Put aside any doubts you might have and ignore the words of those who mock or criticise. Trust in your judgement and everything will work out fine.'

She hovered in front of them in eerie silence.

Ella forgot about her suspicions. 'Can you help me find my mum and dad?'

Seraphina's eyes widened. 'You've lost them?'

'They disappeared six months ago.' Ella stopped herself from grasping at her chest. Her fingers went to her necklace instead. 'The police couldn't find them, though I don't think they really tried. Maybe you could.'

'Witches can do anything,' Billy whispered at Ella's side.

Seraphina drifted over them and settled on to a piece of the ruined priory wall. She stood tall and surveyed the surroundings.

'Location spells are hard, especially with nothing to go on. Unless you have something of theirs I can use?'

Ella removed the chain from her neck. 'My mother gave me this.'

Seraphina twiddled her fingers. The necklace floated from Ella's hand and flew towards the witch, who caught it expertly. Ella's heart pounded against her ribs in expectation. Silence engulfed the three of them for an eternity.

Then Seraphina threw the silver butterfly at Ella. Surprised by the action, Ella failed to catch it. It landed in the dirt. Billy scooped it up and gave it to her.

The witch dropped to the ground and strode towards them.

'It's not strong enough, and neither am I at the moment.'

Ella fought back the disappointment. 'I understand.'

'Would you like to go to the gateway now?' Ella nodded,

and all of them disappeared with one wave of the witch's hand. 'How I've missed the scent of the sea,' Seraphina said as the group arrived at the cliffs.

Billy's feet gave way in the crumbling mud, his legs buckling as he cried out. He fell over the edge, and Ella screamed.

13 SERAPHINA

Ella's eyes bulged like eggs wobbling in a pan of boiling water. She watched as Billy fell into the gap between the clifftop and the sky. Her heart sank as he plummeted towards the sea. She rushed to the edge as the agony coursed through her and gasped at the sight.

'Billy!' She shouted as his body floated in mid-air. His arms and legs swayed in the wind as Ella reached the edge, pulling back before she fell over.

Seraphina stretched her hand towards Billy. Then she reeled him in like a dangling fish on a rod. She closed her fingers into a fist when he was over dry land and he dropped to the ground next to Ella's shoes.

'No need to thank me,' she said.

'Ouch,' Billy shouted.

'You can't get away that easy.'

Ella grabbed Billy's arm and pulled him into the safety of the grass. He laughed as they tumbled over, falling and giggling as they bowled towards Seraphina's feet. The relief sparked joy in Ella's heart.

Billy couldn't stop smiling. 'I flew like a spuggy.' He rolled through the dirt. 'That was exciting and scary as hell.'

Ella gripped on to her belly. 'For both of us.'

He held on to her as they stood. 'What will you do with the unicorn?'

Ella hadn't given it any thought beyond getting the animal to safety.

Seraphina stared at the setting sun. 'You should give her some of your Light.'

'Won't I harm her as the others did at the hospital?'

Ella didn't want to hurt the unicorn. When she'd done it earlier, everything had been fine, but she was worried doing it again too soon could damage the Elemental.

'That was different because they were scavengers. There were too many of them around her,' Seraphina replied. 'They were sucking her dry like vampires. And you're unlike all the others.'

Ella brushed the mud from her legs. 'How am I different?'

Seraphina gazed at Ella. 'You're different because you're the bookkeeper.' The witch strode towards the mystery house as the two kids scrambled behind. The unicorn trotted by their side. 'Can you feel the changes happening, in the sea, in the air, and the earth?' She knelt and ran her fingers through the ground. 'Even here, away from urban decay, a sense of corruption is overwhelming.' She shivered as she stood, dirt dropping from her hand. 'Look at all this senseless destruction.' Seraphina wiped a tear from her eye. 'Maybe you should let all the Elementals through so they retrieve what was theirs and save the world from further devastation.' The witch peered into Ella's soul. 'It couldn't be any worse than what man has done to this beautiful planet and the creatures on it.'

'If I did that, what would happen to all the people?'

The witch's glare made Ella nervous. She owed Seraphina a favour, but if she asked her to release every creature from the book, what would she do?

'You reap what you sow.' Seraphina strode towards the door of the house.

'Where is she going?' Billy said.

Ella followed Seraphina. 'You can't see the building, Billy?'

The unicorn, who appeared weary and had lost some of the sparkle from its eyes, joined her. She placed her arms around its neck and hugged it. It differed from the first time she'd touched it; now, she sensed energy flowing in the other direction. It didn't make her weak, but she knew the unicorn was getting stronger.

Billy gazed into space. 'There's nothing there.'

As he peered across the grass, Seraphina took a step forward, her hand outstretched, and then vanished. Billy gulped as Ella let go of the unicorn, grabbed hold of his arm and pulled the boy close to her.

'Listen, she may have helped us, but I don't trust her. Keep an eye on her at all times.'

'You can use the book to send her back.'

'I promised I wouldn't.' She told him everything that had happened at the hospital.

'Dotty Twist is back to normal again?' He didn't sound happy about it.

'I'm not sure if normal is the right word, but she's out of the coma.'

The thought of her cousin triggered concern for her missing friend.

'I hope Dora's okay.'

Billy scraped bits of mud from the bottom of his trousers.

'If I go home with dirty kecks, me ma will tan my hide.'

He spat into his hands and rubbed them against the dirtiest parts.

Ella put her hand on his shoulder. 'Do you know what happened to Dora?'

His eyes drooped, his voice quiet and trembling.

'She got pushed out of the way when the crowd swarmed around us. I didn't see her after that. I was too busy trying to keep them from crawling on top of the unicorn.'

Ella stared at the animal. She had to believe Dora was safe and had gone home, wherever that was. She led the unicorn inside as Seraphina peered into the box where Ella had found the book. She turned to speak to Billy, but he wasn't there.

'The boy can't enter what he can't see. Not without your help.' Seraphina approached the unicorn as Ella stepped outside. Billy's astonished gaze greeted her.

His eyes bulged. 'You vanished.'

She grabbed his arm. 'Now, I'm back.'

Ella dragged him into the house. As she did so, Seraphina conjured up hay and oats for the unicorn.

'I'm stronger inside here.'

'How can you do these things?' Ella said as the unicorn snacked.

'I can manipulate the particles which exist between Light to move items from one place to another.' Seraphina waved her hands in the air and an apple appeared from nowhere to drop into her palm. She took a bite from it, her strange eyes glowing as she tasted the fruit. 'You don't know how such simple things can be so glorious.' Bits of apple fell from her teeth as she spoke.

'What did you mean when you said somebody created all life? Were you talking about God?'

Ella wanted to learn more about the book and the other world. The idea of a Supreme Being both excited and scared her.

Seraphina stuck out her lips and blew at them.

'Of course not. Your modern religions are childish usurpers compared to the real Creator.' She finished the apple and threw the core to the unicorn.

'God doesn't exist?' Billy appeared distressed by the prospect. It made Ella realise how little she knew about him.

'The Creator of all life is female.' The witch spoke to them as if she was a teacher and they were her newest pupils. 'She made humans and Elementals at the same time. Females first, and then males, Her imagination running wild with each successive creation.'

'This isn't what they teach us in religious education classes,' Billy said. 'God created humans in His image.'

'You've been taught a lie, boy.' Seraphina spoke with such anger, Ella feared she might do something terrible to Billy. She moved closer to him and held his hand. 'Your entire world exists upon deceit and betrayal.'

Seraphina put her arms at her sides. Ella's eyes were drawn to the witch's fingers, noticing how they shook and how she tried to hide the motion.

She trembles as I do.

'What do you mean?' Ella said.

'The Goddess trusted Her creations and man tricked Her into exile.'

Ella considered what she'd just heard.

'Wouldn't that be Her fault for creating such devious people?'

'And Her fault for creating evil Elementals?' Billy added.

Seraphina lifted a couple of inches above the ground and floated towards him.

'The Goddess didn't create good or bad humans, or good or bad Elementals. Living creatures make their own choices.' She leant into Billy's face. 'Do you have bullies in your school, child?'

He gulped and stepped backwards. 'Ye-es,' he stuttered.

'They weren't born that way. They choose to behave like that. Some people and Elementals enjoy inflicting pain on others. The Goddess was ashamed of Her flawed creations. It was this which allowed mankind to trick her. She thought She was doing the right thing by removing the most powerful Elementals from the humans they terrified. But we all suffered for Her mistake.'

The sadness in Seraphina's voice shook Ella. 'Where is this Goddess now?'

Seraphina glided towards the exit.

'Nobody knows. She vanished inside the other realm as the rest of us came to terms with our new prison.' She pushed the door open and peered on to the cliffs. 'I will never return to that place.' The wind moved the hair across her face. 'So I must thank you, Ella Finn, for releasing me. This is farewell until we meet again.'

She waved her fingers at Ella before floating out to sea. Ella and Billy ran out and gazed at her departing figure.

'Where are you going?' Ella shouted at her.

'You'll see me again when I return for the debt you owe me.'

With those words, the witch vanished into the clouds.

'What do we do now?' Billy said as the wind picked up and blew sand into their faces.

'I have to get home.' Ella stroked the unicorn and closed the door of the house. 'And so should you.'

She wanted to see how Dotty was doing. And maybe the sisters would stop picking on her after what she'd done for her injured cousin.

They ran along the cliffs and back to the town as the sun disappeared behind purple clouds. The rain came in hard bursts before violently transforming into thick hailstones. The house was close by as ice smacked into Ella. The air growled around them as she pulled Billy towards the barn. Lighting cracked through the sky as they stumbled into Ella's makeshift living space. The horses cried out as she slammed the door closed.

'Where did that come from?' Billy wiped the water from his face. 'Do you think the witch did it?'

'No.' Ella grabbed a towel from the bed and bent her head into it. She squeezed the rain from her hair. 'It's pressure from the other realm on the weakness in nature. It'll only get worse unless I can stop it.'

She removed the book from her pocket, expecting it to be soaked, surprised it was dryer than the desert.

'How will you do that?' Billy glanced around the barn.

'I could wait for my guide to arrive.'

But there was a plan brewing in her mind, and she didn't think she'd have time to wait. The noise of the hailstones battering the building disappeared as quickly as the manic weather had appeared. Ella opened the door to peer outside. The sun had reappeared, and the wind and rain had gone.

'You should get home, Billy, in case it comes back.'

He took another look around her home.

'Do you sleep in here?' Surprise consumed his face.

'Better that than in there with the rest of them.' She nodded towards the house as they left the barn. 'I'll see you at school tomorrow.'

She strode towards the house. Billy waved at her with a massive grin as he ran into town. The book was in her pocket, pressed up against her body.

I don't need to wait for somebody to show me how to use this.

Her fingers slipped into her clothes to touch the front cover.

I've proved I know what to do with it.

Ella glanced into the sky where the witch had floated away. She knew how she'd save the environment and protect the world.

All she had to discover was which Elemental could find her parents.

14 THE GODDESS

Voices came from the kitchen as Ella burst through the front door. She made sure her shoes were clean and walked in, nervous feet creeping on to the tiles. Dolly, Daisy and Aunt Ida glared at her as if she was a bug under a microscope. There was no sign of Dotty or Uncle George.

Did I dream the whole thing? Is Dotty still in the coma?

Ella clutched at the book in her pocket. For a second, she believed it was an ordinary paperback and nothing else. She slipped her fingers inside and touched the illustrations on the cover, finding the dragon and, for an instant, picturing the beast in her mind. She snatched her hand away at once, panicking about what she might have done. A fierce gust of wind smacked into the outside of the house. She jumped and stared at her cousins.

'There's been a miracle, Ella.' Ida continued to chop the vegetables. 'Dotty has recovered from her coma.'

Ella sighed, relief washing over her. 'Where is she?'

Her aunt thrust carrots under the tap to wash the pesticides off them.

'The doctors wanted to keep her overnight for observation. Just to make sure there's no relapse or after-effects from her condition.' Ida's hand shook as she opened the fridge. 'There are no eggs left.'

Ida's mind appeared to be a million miles away. Ella recognised the shock written across her aunt's face.

'Don't worry, Ma.' Dolly stood. 'Me and Ella will get fresh ones from the hens.' Before Ella could protest, Dolly dragged her outside. There was a trace of electricity in the air from the recent freak weather. Dolly dug her nails into Ella's arm and shoved her against the wall. The wind howled around them as Ella tried to ignore the pain.

'I need to make sure my ma is okay, but tomorrow, after school, you'll tell me how you did it,' Dolly growled at her. 'You'll explain what that book is and how to use it.' She pulled the book from Ella's trousers as her other hand gripped her throat. 'I'll keep this with me and you'll do as you're told this time.'

Ella struggled to breathe. 'You'll ruin everything.'

If she lost the book to Dolly, she might never see it again.

Dolly glared at her cousin and released her grip.

'What do you mean?'

Ella's breathing returned to normal. Inside her head, cogs clicked into place as her brain worked overtime.

'If I don't keep it with me, all will be reversed. If you take it, Dotty will fall back into a coma.' She peered into her cousin's eyes. 'And it'll be your fault.'

Energy crackled in the air. The gulls squawked in the sky as Ella's heart bounced against her ribs. Dolly stared at her as if she'd reach down and rip Ella's lungs up through her throat.

She dropped the book to the ground.

'Get the eggs,' she snarled. 'We'll sort this tomorrow.'

Ella's legs wobbled against the wall as her cousin returned to the house. She bent to get the book, her fingers trembling against the cover.

I know how I'll fix everything.

She strode to the hatchery. Ella had her plan, and nothing would stop her from putting it into action.

Ella spent the rest of the night in limited conversation with her family, enduring her cousins' glaring eyes. She went to bed early, so excited about her plans, she didn't notice Ratter wasn't there when she returned to the barn.

———

ELLA WOKE EARLIER than usual the next day, missing breakfast and her chores to check on the unicorn in the mystery house. She ran along the cliffs as fast as she could, skipping through the grass and enjoying the warmth of the sun. The weather appeared to have settled down into something resembling normality.

The sight of the building standing dark against the daylight made her smile. She had thirty minutes to spare before heading back and going to school.

But I can't stay in there for half an hour because it's four hours out here.

She did a quick calculation in her head.

Only three minutes inside.

Unless she wanted to get into trouble again.

She found the timer app on her phone, set it for three minutes and hit the start button as she pushed the door open.

The unicorn's gentle snores greeted her as she crept into the house. She knelt by its side, placing her hand on its back, feeling the Light flowing from her and into the unicorn, and vice versa. Ella needed to know how this worked, what Seraphina meant by a symbiosis between humans and Elementals. She placed her fingers on its chest, the rhythm of its breathing creating peace throughout Ella.

She lay like that for sixty seconds before rising and opening the book. Ella had two minutes left in the house.

Books should have words in them.

Ella stared at the pictures of the unicorn, the pixie and the witch. The sight of the pixie reminded her of Dora, and she hoped her new friend was okay. She turned the first page and ran her fingers over the next one; it was like touching the skin of a tortoise.

Maybe there are words here, but I can't see them.

Ella pressed her hand into the paper.

'How do you work?'

She focused on the page. Nothing happened.

'Who created you?' No response.

'Who is the Goddess?' Still nothing.

'Where are my parents?' No answer.

'Why can I use the book, but nobody else can?'

Nothing happened. She dropped it on the floor in frustration and the noise woke the unicorn. It sprang to its feet with ease and strode towards her, nestling its head at the back of her neck and licking Ella's skin. She giggled at the touch, banishing the irritation from her mind and stroking its hair.

'It seems wrong to give you a name, but I suppose I should.' Ella gazed into the unicorn's eyes as she considered it. 'How does Star sound, girl?'

Ella patted its back. It purred like a kitten, and she took that as an acceptance of its new title.

She returned her attention to the blank pages of the book for another try.

'What is Light?'

The paper shimmered under her touch and she lifted her hand from the page. Dark cursive letters appeared as if inked by invisible fingers. She gripped her palms as the writing crossed from one page and into the next before stopping. Star licked at her cheek as the alarm on her phone went off. She kissed the unicorn goodbye and stepped out of the house.

Ella read the first paragraph aloud.

'Light is the matter which binds all life. It is the nourishment of existence. It flows between all things, handed down by the Creator of all things. Life can exist in the absence of Light, but without it, there is only the hollow of the abyss: and from the abyss flow anger, hatred, malice and despair.'

Ella thought about those words before studying the rest of the text. She read about the sharing of Light between living creatures, the importance of consensual sharing and the devastation of taking Light by force or greed. She glanced at her phone and guessed she had twenty minutes to get to school before the bell rang for the start of the day. But she'd changed her mind about that.

I don't care about school.

She ran out with no intention of going to her classes, but she wanted to catch Billy and Dora before they went inside. She had to see if they were both okay, especially Dora. Ella sprinted as fast as she could, the sun scorching her skin as she dashed along the cliffs, past the Twist home, and on the way to the playground. Ella wished Seraphina was there to whisk her through that journey in an instant, but she was both intrigued and wary of the witch.

I'm going to melt.

She tugged at the top of her shirt and undid the first few buttons. It was summer, but it shouldn't have been so hot.

She galloped past people who were wilting in the heat and struggling to find the comfort of some shade.

The school gates were ahead of her when the bell rang. Ella wiped the sweat from her head and wondered why she didn't have either of her friends' phone numbers. All the kids disappeared inside before she reached the entrance. She pulled up and dodged behind some bushes before the teachers on duty spotted her.

'Crap.' She lay on the ground and moved into the shadows.

'Is that any way for a young lady to speak?'

It was a familiar voice above her. She stared into the haze of the sun and the outline of Billy Pudding.

He dropped to the floor and rolled next to her.

'It's like being stuck inside an oven in the desert.'

'Why aren't you in school, Billy?'

'He didn't go because I told him to wait for you.'

Joy leapt into Ella's heart at the sound of Dora's voice. She pushed herself from the ground and grabbed the other girl.

'I thought something bad might've happened to you outside the hospital.'

Relief flowed through Ella.

'The mob crowded me out and shoved me to one side. When I got up, you'd all gone.' Dora narrowed her eyes. 'Billy told me you had help from a witch.'

The words struggled out of Dora as Ella kept on squeezing. She stopped when Billy got to his feet.

'Yes,' Ella said as she let go. 'There's a lot to tell you.'

Sweat dripped from Dora in waves. 'Can we find somewhere cooler than this?'

'The weather is crazy.' Billy rolled up his sleeves and used them to wipe his face.

Ella watched both of them struggling to cool down.

'The wall between this world and the Elemental one is breaking down. Poison, pollution, chemicals, plastic: these things are weakening the barrier. I think I know how to stop it.'

'How can you do that?' Billy asked.

'Let's head down to the beach,' Ella said. 'It'll be cooler there, and we can hide under the pier.' They nodded in unison, put their hands over their heads, and made their way to the coast while trying to avoid the blaze of the sun. People flopped on the streets as the kids rushed through the town. They ran down the bank in a frenzy, unable to control their forward movement as gravity pulled them closer to the water. Ella thought her shoes would melt into the ground.

'Thank the Goddess.' The sea breeze settled on her face as they raced under the steel legs of the pier. She dipped her feet in the waves lapping the beach.

'I heard what you just said.' Billy headed for the shade. 'You believe everything the witch told you?'

Ella rubbed at her chin. 'I don't know.'

'Maybe we should ask Dora.' Billy stared at her. 'You know a lot about the book. What about this Goddess story the witch told us?'

Dora joined Ella in the sea. The waves drifted over Ella's shoes, seeping through the top and over the sides and cooling her skin. Dora kicked at the water.

'My parents mentioned nothing about that. But they said it was the old gods who ruled the planet long before the new ones came along. Mother said they were invented idols, created by men to control the world.'

'Why would they do that?' Confusion crept over Billy's face.

Ella had given it considerable thought.

'If a female god created this planet and everything on it, including the Elementals, then perhaps men didn't like that. Maybe they banished everything stronger than them and rewrote the facts to suit themselves: Her story became His story.'

She still basked in the cooler temperature.

'That sounds silly.' Billy ran his fingers through the sea.

'You would think that,' Dora said. 'You're a boy.'

Ella stared at her phone. 'Holy crap.'

Since Seraphina had whisked them away, she'd not had time to check the news or her social media until now. She watched the video clip of her, Billy, Seraphina and the unicorn vanishing outside the hospital. There were already over a million views of it online.

'What's wrong?' Dora said.

Ella showed it to them. 'We're in trouble now.'

15 THE BIG BANG

'Did you see this?' Ella showed her phone to the others. 'Yeah, I went through all the comments last night,' Billy said as Dora nodded.

Ella flicked through the news, posts and video clips. She played the bit where they disappeared from the hospital grounds and Seraphina transported them to the cliffs. The consensus from those who weren't there was the whole thing was a hoax and fake news. She didn't know what to make of that.

Billy stood next to her. 'Did you read the quotes from some of the patients?'

She scanned down the screen until she found what he meant.

'Those who touched Star are claiming they got better. They say they feel healthier now.'

It amazed Ella how many people thought the clip was a stunt.

'Who's Star?' Billy said. She explained about naming the unicorn.

'Excellent choice,' Dora said.

'Humans can improve their health from touching an Elemental?' Ella asked Dora.

'Apparently so.' Dora brushed a stray hair from her eyes.

'What happened to the pixie?' Ella peered at Dora.

'She's safe and sound.' Dora removed the small creature from her pocket. 'Once those people went crazy at the hospital, I had to hide this girl away.'

'Can you let Billy hold her?'

An idea had formed in Ella's head. Her new friend shrugged and handed the pixie to the boy. He smiled as he held out his hand and the small Elemental dropped on to his skin and beamed at him. It danced a little jig in his palm, spinning around and jumping into the air before finishing with a pirouette.

'How do you feel?' Ella said to him.

Billy grinned at her. 'Thrilled, like, the happiest I've ever been.' He sat down in the dunes as the pixie performed another dance on his hand. 'It tickles.'

He let it go on to the beach where it danced and played in the sand, using its fingers to write in an unknown language.

'Yes!' Ella shouted as she twirled in the water. 'This confirms everything I thought. You two need to help me with my plan.'

She bopped in the sea while the others stared at her in bemusement.

'What are you on about?' Billy stood as the pixie grinned at him.

Ella took both of their hands and dragged them further into the shade.

'It was on my mind all last night. How I can bring good Elementals into our world and repair the damage to the environment and strengthen the barrier against the other realm.'

Their eyes were as wide as their mouths. She told them about the questions she'd asked of the book.

Billy arched his eyebrows at her. 'What do you mean?'

'Every living thing is made of Light. That Light has been worn away over the last century, destroyed by what humanity has done to the planet. We need to replace the Light to restore the balance between all things.'

With all her heart, Ella knew what she'd thought about all night, what she was telling them, was right. Human pollution was destroying the Light. There was nothing three kids in a small English town could do about that, but she was convinced they could do something about replacing the lost Light.

A bemused expression crossed Billy's face. 'Where does this Light come from?'

'It came from the Creator,' Ella replied. 'It came from the Goddess.'

'But where did she come from?' His eyes were on stalks.

'She created Herself,' Dora added.

'That's impossible,' Billy sneered. 'You can't create something like that.'

'So how do you explain all religions and their gods? Where did God come from?' Ella stared at him. 'Or what about the Big Bang, how did that happen? How did that explosion happen?'

Billy spluttered in utter confusion.

'I don't know. I never pay attention in RE or science classes.'

'Well, I do.' Ella shook her head at him. Her mother had explained this many times, so she knew it by heart. 'Most astronomers believe the universe began in a Big Bang. The entire cosmos was inside a bubble that was thousands of times smaller than a pinhead. It was hotter and denser than anything we can imagine.'

'Was it as hot as this crazy weather?'

Billy took off his shirt. She tried not to stare at the ragged vest he wore.

Ella continued. 'Then, it exploded. The universe we know was born. Time, space and matter all began with the Big Bang. In a fraction of a second, the cosmos grew from smaller than a single atom to bigger than a galaxy. And it kept on growing at a fantastic rate. It's still expanding today. Perhaps what scientists think of as the Big Bang was the creation of this Goddess from that first explosion.'

'If that's the case, why do all religions say God is a man?'

Ella shook her head. 'That's not true. Some people believe God to be the Supreme Being that doesn't have a body, neither male nor female.'

Billy's face was a jigsaw puzzle missing most of the pieces.

'Did you learn that in class?'

She smiled at him. 'Yes, in my first year at my previous school.'

The memory of it made her think of her parents. Ella never stopped thinking about them, they were always in her mind somewhere, but she'd been able to control the pain. She couldn't now and the sadness came flooding back.

'So, what's your plan?' Dora said as Billy continued to look flabbergasted.

'I'll use the book to summon Elementals to repair the damage to the earth, the sea and the air. And I'll bring others, the good ones, to live in harmony with humans; to give joy and good health like Star and the pixie have done.'

She had complete faith in her plan. 'I'll bring back the symbiosis of living things. But I'll need your help to do it.'

Ella's new friends gawped at her.

'That's the stupidest thing I've ever heard, and the most dangerous.' Ella turned her head as a heavy foot kicked her into the ground. 'But at least your stupidity allowed me to find the book my ancestors have searched over two thousand years for.'

Ella spat sand from her lips and glared at her attacker. He appeared to be a few years older than them, maybe eighteen, with a severe haircut making him look like an army recruit. There was a tinge to his accent, which made her think he was Irish.

'What do you want?'

She got to her feet. Dora and Billy stood by her side, the three of them standing together against any more attacks.

'I'm here to show you how to use that.'

He pointed at the book sticking out of her pocket. Ella gulped at his words. Was he the teacher she was told to expect? She tried not to smile at him, remembering the kick he'd just given her.

'You know how to do that?'

The stranger reached inside his jacket and removed a small piece of wood. He tapped it in the palm of his hand and it unfolded to six feet long.

'This staff is older than this country. Do you recognise the carvings covering it?'

He held it out and twirled it in front of Ella as she stared at the images.

'They're Elementals.' She also noticed the bracelet on the stranger's wrist.

He peered at her. 'Do you know what Light is?' Ella

nodded. 'Good. This staff is carved from Light and it's deadly to all Elementals, even the strongest of them.'

Dora scowled at him. 'What do you want?'

He finished showing off his skills and addressed them.

'I'll tell the child how to destroy the book.'

Pain shot through Ella's chest on hearing his words.

'Why would I do that?'

He planted the staff in the sand. 'Don't you want to save the world from destruction?'

'Of course,' Ella replied.

'Then destroying the book will do that by preventing all the monsters from coming here.'

She shook her head at him. 'They'll still come through when the changes in the climate destroy the barrier.'

He laughed at her. 'That'll never happen. None of it will make any difference because the book's destruction will kill all Elementals regardless of where they are. But only you can do it.'

'I won't do that.' Ella glared at him.

'Are you sure?' Before she could reply, he lunged forward, grabbing Billy by the throat and dragging him from the girls. 'How many people do I need to kill before you do as I say?' Billy struggled in the stranger's grasp as the older boy forced his head under his arm. 'I could squash your friend like a peanut.'

Ella fought to control her breathing as the stranger loosened his grip on Billy and pushed him forward by the neck.

'Leave him alone.'

He placed the staff into Billy's back.

'One small nudge from me and this will cut him in half.' Billy whimpered as his assailant gripped him tighter. 'I'll push his guts all over this beach and turn the sand red.'

Ella didn't hesitate. 'Release him and I'll do what you want.'

Her grip increased on the book as he laughed at her.

'No. You do what I say, and then I let him go. If you don't, he dies, and your other friend is next.' He glared at Dora.

A great weight surged through Ella as she nodded. 'Good girl.' His smirk sent daggers through her heart. 'You need to return the creatures you brought here to the other realm before you destroy it. Otherwise, they'll be stuck with us.' He pulled his arm and the staff back so it wasn't touching Billy. 'Do that first.'

Ella glanced at the book and knew what to do. She tried to ignore the fear in Billy's eyes and the tension running through her limbs. She placed her shaking fingers over the image of the witch, remembering the promise she'd made to Seraphina. Ella tilted the front cover up so the stranger couldn't see what she was doing.

'Who are you?'

He pursed his lips and arched his eyebrows at her.

'My name is Kylian and I'm the latest in a long line of guardians, a protector of our way of life against those creatures from the other realm.'

Ella dismissed his arrogance and pride.

'It was your ancestors who tricked the Goddess into sending the Elementals away.'

He hunched his shoulders and sneered at her.

'There's no such thing as a Goddess. There are only those monsters who do the Devil's work. And you're one of them, but you'll remove them from existence forever. Have you sent the others back?'

Ella ignored his question.

'Show me the page,' he shouted. She held it up to him as

the shadow at his back grew to reach the rafters of the pier. 'What have you done?' He peered at the fourth illustration.

'You should've brought a slingshot with you.' Ella jumped to the side as the cyclops reached down and snatched Kylian from Billy. He tossed the man and his staff into the dunes as if they were nothing.

'Are you okay?' Ella ran to her friend. The poor boy was gazing at the one-eyed giant and trembling.

Dora joined them. 'We have to get away from here.'

Kylian was already picking himself up from the sand and snarling in their direction. Ella summoned all her courage and took the cyclops by the hand and spoke to it.

'Keep him busy, but don't hurt him too much.'

She remembered what the knocker had done to Dotty. The Elemental's single eye stared right at her as it reached for her throat.

That's when Ella knew she'd made a terrible mistake.

16 ELEMENTALS

The cyclops stopped, its large arm frozen in front of her face. Ella's hands shook, but so did the creature's. It gazed at her hands, watching them tremble as confusion consumed its eye. Ella held her fingers up and took his into hers.

'I'll help you,' she whispered, 'but I need your help first.' Their hands trembled together, with Ella's smaller one encased inside his. 'Will you do what I ask?' Their eyes met as their flesh parted. The cyclops grunted and strode towards the Irishman. 'And keep away from that staff,' Ella added as she dragged Billy into the scorching sunlight.

Billy shielded his face from the sun. 'You can control him?'

Ella pulled him from the pier. 'I wasn't sure if he'd listen, but I think perhaps the more primitive Elementals will do as I say. Seraphina, the witch, wouldn't.'

'Ouch,' Dora said as the cyclops swatted the stranger into the sand again with one massive sweep of his impressive arm.

'This weather is unbearable, but at least the heat is

keeping most people indoors.' Ella glanced around the beach and the bank leading into town. 'I don't think we can keep hoping that stuff like this will go down as fake news.'

'We need to get you and the book away from this stranger,' Dora said as they headed off the sand.

'How did he find us?' Billy said as all three of them placed their hands above their heads. They dashed through the edge of the sea for relief from the sun.

Water splashed on to Ella's yellow and black socks.

'I don't know. Maybe it has something to do with the book.'

'Did you notice the bracelet on his wrist?' Dora said. Both the others nodded as they ran. 'Elemental symbols covered it, and they changed all the time like an animation.'

They continued running, picking up speed to reach the far end of the beach. They scrambled up the sandbank towards the Twist house at the top. When they got there, Ella turned to look at the fight they'd left behind. The cyclops was limping and sluggish.

Dora pointed at them. 'The stranger could kill him with that staff.'

Sadness overwhelmed Ella at the thought she might have got the Elemental killed so they could escape. She opened the book and pressed her finger into the cyclops image.

'Go back,' she said and imagined him vanishing. As she stared down at the legs of the pier, he did just that. The Irishman swung his staff at empty air. 'Come on. We'll hide in the mystery house.'

They scampered past the barn and the Twist home, keeping low to avoid detection from any of Ella's relatives. The sun beat down on the short grass which lined most of the cliff. Some potholes had sprung up since she was there last, and the three of them had to dodge and jump over the dangerous obstructions. Ella was glad to see the house up ahead of them. She took Billy and Dora by the hand and pulled them into the building.

'Hello, Star.'

She closed the door behind them and Billy threw himself into the straw for a lie-down. Ella patted Star before heading to the window, peering out to check if they'd been followed.

'What do we do now?' Dora was at her side. 'We can't stay here forever.'

Ella ran her fingers over the sunburnt skin on her arm, gazing through the glass as the heat scorched the earth. She stared into the sea as giant waves rushed towards the beach. Taller than the cyclops, they tossed the surfers high into the air. Ella wondered how long the planet's climate had left before it cracked and everything on the other side came tumbling through.

'The Irishman will discover us soon enough once we're out of here.' Ella wandered over to Star and touched the horn on her head. 'So, I don't have a lot of time. I have to put my plan into action now.' She pulled the book from her pocket and ran her hands over the images on both covers. 'But I'm not sure if I have the strength to summon what we need to fix things.'

Somewhere deep in the back of her mind, she still wondered if, in time, it would be possible to use the book to find her parents. The witch couldn't do it, but perhaps another Elemental could.

Dora's voice snapped the thought from her head.

'You'll have our strength.'

Dora held on to her hand. Ella smiled as they sat in front of the box where she'd found the book not so long ago.

Billy sat on Ella's other side. 'How will it work?'

Ella took a large gulp and breathed through her nose.

'Pollution has weakened the Light which binds the planet's atmosphere, upsetting the stability of nature. That Light needs replacing to repair the damage, just like Star healed some patients at the hospital, so I need to summon Elementals to heal our world.'

She'd spent all night thinking about it. It was the only thing which made sense when she thought how she'd stumbled into the house nobody else could see.

Billy pointed at the book. 'Is someone still coming to show you how to use that?'

Ella gripped his hand to calm his nerves.

'I think everyone I've met in the last few days has shown me what to do regarding it. Dora provided knowledge, Seraphina offered me confidence and the stranger who attacked us gave me urgency. And you, Mr Billy Pudding, provided hope.'

Dora smiled at her. 'Hope is all you need.'

Ella peered at the images on the book for the thousandth time.

'That and the strongest Elementals I can summon.'

Dora continued to hold on to Ella's hand. 'Which will you choose?'

Ella took another deep breath and gathered her thoughts.

'We need Elementals for the earth, the sea, and the air.'

'What about fire?' Billy shivered in the house's atmosphere.

Ella giggled and grinned at him. 'See, Billy, I knew you'd remember something from science classes.' She was happy to watch him rediscover his smile.

'The Light is fire. We want enough to restore the other three.'

Ella moved her free hand over the front cover. Her nerves tingled with excitement as a loud bang outside shook them.

'It's too late.'

She jumped up and ran to the window.

Billy trembled next to the unicorn. 'What is it?'

Dora stood next to Ella. 'There's nothing there.'

Ella pushed her face against the mysterious glass as something large bounced off it. She flinched backwards, neck turning as her body tumbled towards the ground. Dora caught her and pulled Ella up as another object hit the window.

'The Irishman is here,' Ella said as Kylian came into view with his staff pointing at the door. She couldn't start her plan while he was outside. Ella scanned the back cover of the book and found a creature with the body, tail, and legs of a lion, plus the head and wings of an eagle: a gryphon.

She placed her finger on the picture. 'Come now and take him away, remove the man with the staff far from here, but do not harm him.'

She gazed from the window as she spoke. Kylian strode towards the house as the air shimmered above his head. Large talons came from nothing and grabbed him by his jacket. The gryphon appeared and flew high above the field as the Irishman struggled against his captor. They disappeared into the distance as Ella prepared herself.

'I need to do this now.' Ella turned and pulled Dora into a sitting position. She placed her palm on the book again and found the image she wanted. 'I'll start with the air.'

Dora gripped her hand. 'What will you summon?'

'Pegasus,' Ella replied.

A confused look crept over Billy's face.

'Why Pegasus? What can one flying horse do?'

'Every Elemental belongs to a species.' Ella didn't know how she knew, but she did. 'There'll be hundreds of flying horses to cross the world and deliver Light back to the skies.' She gripped Dora's hand and pressed her finger into the image of the winged stallion. 'Bring them all, bring your family.'

Ella's fingers shook, but it wasn't because of fear or anxiety; this time, it was through energy flowing from her to the book and vice versa.

'I can hear them,' Billy shouted as he ran to the window.

The two girls followed him and stared at something magnificent. As far as the eye could see, pale wings rose from the mist above the sea and soared into the air. There were hundreds of them lifting off and scattering amongst the clouds.

Ella's heart thumped with joy.

'Spread your Light across the world,' she said to their departing bodies.

'The Irishman hasn't returned.' Dora sounded concerned.

'Maybe the gryphon squashed him.' Billy laughed.

Ella pressed the book against the window and grabbed Dora's hand.

'Let's go.' Ella pulled Dora through the door. She had no fear of what was there; no worry the stranger with the staff would attack them. Confidence surged through Ella. 'I'll deal with anything that comes our way.'

Billy stepped outside, the sound of beating wings hovering above them in the sky.

'Is it the earth or sea next?' Dora said as Ella dragged her towards the cliffs.

The two girls sat down and Ella peered at the images of the Elementals. Her fingers fell on to the illustration she wanted, her mind reaching out to the creatures she needed. Billy joined them on the edge. The oppressive heat had decreased and a fresh breeze cooled them.

'Look!' Ella pointed towards the sea. Billy gazed in astonishment while Dora smirked at the dozens of large fins bursting from the water.

'Mermaids!' Billy yelled. They soared through the ocean, their long hair blowing in the wind before they fell below the waves and out of sight.

'Swim far and wide, far and deep,' Ella said.

'Earth next,' Dora said.

Ella gazed at the book and wondered what to choose. On the last row of the front cover, she found what she wanted. She pressed her finger into the image.

'The ground is shaking,' Billy cried.

Ella looked around them as small hands poked up from the dirt. She grinned as the gnomes crawled up through the mud and grass and scattered across the cliff. There were hundreds.

'This is happening all over the world,' Ella said.

A surge of electricity tingled through her body. The changes to the environment were already occurring; she could feel them. It would take months or years to repair the climate, but it had begun. She'd started it.

Billy put a hand to his face. 'It's amazing.'

Ella stared into the sea, the happiest she'd been since coming to this town. She still had to deal with the strange Irishman, but now she was proud of what she'd done. It would be useless to fight him and she didn't want to put another Elemental at risk. The only way to handle Kylian was to talk to him, but she didn't know how she'd do that. And then there were her cousins.

Thunder and lightning lit up the sky like fireworks. Seagulls scattered in the clouds and a group of rabbits scampered through the grass.

Ratter.

She'd forgotten all about the rat in the recent excitement. What was happening would scare the poor thing witless. Ella turned her gaze from the stormy sea.

'I need to get back to the barn.'

She sprinted along the cliff, joy in her heart and a spring in her step. Around her, she saw winged horses, mermaids, and gnomes restoring the Light to the planet. It would take time, but she knew this was the beginning of the rebirth of the earth. It was all she thought about as she dashed across the cliff.

Dora and Billy ran with her. At that moment, with the energy in the atmosphere turning the electric sky a shimmering blue, Ella was invincible. She barged through the door and flicked the lights on, surprised at the illumination blaring from the TV.

Darkness covered her eyes when something thumped the side of her head and Ella slithered to the floor.

17 BARNSTORMING

There was a lump the size of a tangerine on her neck when she woke. Ella spat dirt from her mouth, cleared the haze from her eyes and stared at a nightmare made real.

'Do you know how long we've been waiting for you?'

Dolly grinned, placing thick fingers around Ratter as Dotty stood next to her sister with one arm resting on Dora's shoulders. Daisy held a large kitchen knife to Billy's cheek.

'Yer just in time ta watch me give Pudding a new 'aircut.'

Ella clutched at her chest, legs wobbling as she pushed off the ground. Her mind ached as much as her limbs did. The smell of burnt copper near her head was the blood drying on her skull. An incessant throbbing buzzing echoed inside her brain.

'Is this your doing?' Dolly jabbed at the scenes on the TV. 'Did you and that book do all this?'

'What?'

The ringing in Ella's ears disappeared as she listened to the words coming from the screen.

'Numerous sightings around the world of angels in the sky and devils in the sea have led to some people claiming we are entering the end of times. Scientists are putting the extravagant claims down to a rise in dramatic changes in the atmosphere linked to an increase in solar flares. Social media is also awash with images and videos of the strange phenomena.'

'You'll tell me everything you've done,' Dolly said, 'or I'll squeeze the life from this rat.'

Ella wiped the dirt from her clothes as Billy trembled when the dagger kissed his face. Dora was a picture of calmness, but there was terror in Ratter's little eyes. Ella gulped and scratched at the new lump on her head.

'Do you promise to let Ratter go?'

Dolly nodded in agreement.

Ella told them everything that had happened to her since she got the book. She didn't mention the mystery house, wanting to keep that secret, saying she'd found the book under some rocks. Her cousins gawped at each other in amazement before staring at her.

'You brought a witch out of that book to save my life?'

There was ice in Dotty's voice which hadn't been there before Seraphina dipped her fingers into the girl's skull. Ella guessed Dolly hadn't told Dotty what happened in that hospital room.

Ella stared at Dotty. 'I couldn't leave you like that.'

Dolly dropped Ratter on to the floor. The little rat hurried into the safety of the shadows.

'That's because it was your fault.'

Ella shivered under Dotty's glare.

'Give me the book,' Dolly commanded. Ella hesitated before handing it over. 'This only works for you and you control these creatures?'

Ella nodded. 'Some of them, maybe the more primitive ones, but I couldn't control Seraphina.'

'Why is that?' Dolly said.

Ella shrugged. There was so much she still didn't understand.

Daisy pushed Billy away. 'It's a load of bull.'

Ella sighed with relief to see him safe from that blade.

'It's all true.'

She didn't care if they believed her or not; she had to keep them talking while she figured a way out of this mess.

Daisy scowled at her. 'God created the world, not some Goddess.'

'Centuries of lies,' Dora said to the girl standing next to her.

Dolly had the pages open, looking over the images before checking both covers.

'All of these things exist, like the witch you brought to the hospital?'

Ella nodded. 'These and many more.'

Daisy grinned. 'We'll use it to boss this town.'

Dotty took the book from her sister.

'We can rule more than this place.' She strode around the barn, arms high above her head as if she was a Queen ruling over her Empire. 'We'll have an army of creatures. Dragons and monsters and magnificent beasts doing what we want.'

Darkness seeped out of Dotty which was blacker than the night. She scared Ella, whose legs trembled as the shaking returned to her hands. Ella dug her nails into her palms as hard as she could. The pain forced the fear and confusion from her mind. Blood trickled on to her wrists as she glowered at her cousins.

Dolly nodded and grinned. 'You might prove useful after all, Smella.'

Ella controlled herself. 'You won't get my help with any of that. I need the book to save the world, to repair the damage to the climate. I've already started that tonight, and you won't ruin that.'

'If ya don't do what we tell ya, I'll gut these two.'

Daisy spun the knife between her fingers. As she did so, the horses cried out. A shadow scuttled around the edges of the room. A dark slithering thing jumped from the roof and into the gloom, and Ella flinched. Something was wrong: a disturbance more worrying than her cousins.

'You might need that knife for something else first,' Dora said.

The air turned chilly as a thin mist floated across the ground and edged closer to Ella. She recoiled backwards and her fingers trembled next to her legs.

Her voice shivered. 'There's a monster in the room with us.'

'Spider baby!' Billy shouted as he jumped on to the bed.

The horses bawled as the girls froze.

'How?' Ella said as the creature ran for her.

Its eight limbs sprang from the ground, pushing its fat, slithering body towards Ella's face. Its head was all mangled and twisted, red eyes glaring at her, sharp teeth chomping like a pneumatic drill.

It was inches from her head when the knife plunged into its chest. It split in half as Daisy dragged the blade along the length of its ghastly shape. The two parts of it rolled around and squealed like a dying pig.

'Nothing kills ya but me, Smella.'

Daisy wiped the Elemental blood from the dagger on to her skirt. Ella's legs quaked as she stared at the others.

Dolly grabbed Ella's arm. 'Why did you bring that thing here?'

Ella squirmed in her grasp. 'I didn't.'

Before she could say anything else, a high-pitched scream erupted in the barn. Ella put her hands over her ears and cringed. Something banged against the front door.

Dolly dug her fingers into Ella. 'What have you summoned?'

Ella yelled at her cousin. 'This isn't me.'

The door crashed open and an abomination shrieked in their faces. It walked on two legs with a feathered body like a giant bird. Its wings flapped viciously as it continued to screech through a human head crafted from the pits of Hell. The creature's yellow eyes dripped hate, black teeth pulsing with rancid breath. Its long nails scraped against the ground as it strode for the girls. Its face was haggard with an insatiable hunger.

'It's a harpy.'

Ella grabbed a spade from the rack behind her. The shaking had stopped.

Daisy held the knife out at the monster. 'I'll gut it like a fish.'

The beast lifted into the air, screeching even louder as it flapped towards them. Its talons beat to the same rhythm as its wings, heading straight for Ella's head. She brought the shovel up like a shield, the yellow nails scratching against the metal. The monster pushed down and forced Ella to the ground.

'Another one,' Billy yelled as a second harpy flew into the barn.

It brushed past its sister and headed for him. The harpy's legs were outstretched and aimed at his head, and he froze in fear. The whole place echoed with the sound of the creature's wild screaming. Talons soared towards his eyes as a broomstick smashed into its withered bones. The blow sent it back and upwards into the rafters of the barn.

'You better hide under the bed, Pudding.'

Dolly loomed over him, grasping the broom and staring at the hovering harpy. Billy ignored her advice, got up and ran to Ella. The first beast stood on top of the spade, squashing her into the ground. She struggled to breathe as it draped its long arms either side of the spade protecting her, jabbing at her body and tearing at her clothes. Ella summoned all of her strength to defend herself, her mind focusing on how she could save them all.

If I can get to the book, I could bring other Elementals to help us.

Billy bellowed something unrecognisable as the weight dropped from the shield. He grabbed hold of Ella's arm and dragged her from underneath the spade. Next to her head was the horrible face of the creature which had tried to kill her. Daisy stood over it, cleaning more blood from her knife.

'Nothing kills ya but me.'

Billy pulled Ella up. 'There's still another one over there.'

Ella held the spade above her, ready to smash the monster when it descended. The sight of its dead sister sent the harpy into a manic dive, screeching towards the children as Ella swung the metal as fast as she could. The edge struck the harpy's neck and cut deep. Blood splattered over the barn as the beast spiralled into the dirt. It crawled around in the mud as it died in a howl of noise.

Ella stared at her cousins. 'We make an excellent team.'

Then she dropped the bloodied spade on to the ground.

'Don't get too carried away.' Dolly pointed to the TV. 'How are you going to deal with that?'

Ella stepped over the dead Elemental and gazed in amazement at the screen. Dragons flew in the sky and spewed fire along the coast. The picture cut to somewhere else, mobile phone clips from a yacht floating in the sea. A massive serpent emerged from the water, its back covered in plastic bottles as its vast red tongue snapped towards the people on the vessel and the camera went black. A shocked presenter tried to explain the broadcast, his voice erratic and loud. Ella didn't hear what he said as she watched more clips: a giant wolf running amok in Newcastle; strange skeletal creatures climbing Blackpool Tower; a group of scorpion men scattering the crowds around the Houses of Parliament. She couldn't take anymore, striding over to turn off the television.

'What's happening?'

Billy took hold of her hand. The shaking returned to her fingers as she peered into his scared face.

'I don't know. None of this is my doing.'

Dolly scowled at her. 'I thought you could control these creatures?'

As Ella's cousins stood in a line and glared at her, her mind was a fog of confusion. The attacks had surprised her, but the events across the rest of the country baffled her. Was it all a consequence of what she'd done with the book, bringing over the mermaids, gnomes and flying horses?

She was about to say something when a massive object smacked into the front of the barn. The force of it knocked her to the ground.

'Ella,' Billy cried as her shoulder thumped into stone.

Dust swirled everywhere in the air, covering her eyes and jumping between her lips. She spluttered and coughed as he yanked her upwards.

She wiped the dust from her face. 'What was that?'

A great head pushed its way through the grime floating around them. Its eyes burned yellow and red, with heat drifting from its mouth. A humongous snake-like tongue slithered across the floor, stopping just a few feet from Ella, and she expected her heart to burst.

'Hello, children, have you missed me?'

Seraphina sat on the dragon's back and grinned at them.

18 REVELATIONS

'This is all your doing?' Ella's anger burned out of her and towards the witch.

How could I have been so stupid as to trust her?

'Of course not,' Seraphina replied. 'I serve a higher power. Check your book.'

Seraphina descended from the dragon and patted it on the head. Its eyes glared at the children, burning yellow and red. Ella's inner rage distracted her from the dragon's intense gaze as she snatched the book from Dolly's startled fingers. She flipped the cover open to the first page: all she saw were the Elementals she'd summoned, including the image of the witch.

Ella placed her finger over the illustration. She could break her promise now and not feel guilty about it.

'Don't get any ideas of sending me back.' Seraphina glared at Ella. 'If I disappear, the dragon will scorch everything in sight.'

She'd lost the starched business suit of earlier and replaced it with a long ruby leather jacket, dark boots and skin-tight trousers. It was remarkable she could even walk in them.

Ella pointed to the first page. 'I didn't summon any monsters.'

The dragon growled as the witch examined her nails.

'Turn to the back.'

The dragon's breath stank of rotten eggs and ash. Little spits of fire bubbled from its mouth and scorched the ground. The smell of burning smoke drifted through the barn.

Ella did as instructed, wondering why she'd never checked beyond the front pages apart from the first time she'd discovered the book. The hairs on her neck prickled as she turned to the inside back page, her heart throbbing at the sight of several illustrations, including the dragon, the harpy, and the spider baby. This was impossible.

'But how...?'

Her fingers shivered, and the vibrations travelled beyond her wrist and up her arms until she nearly dropped the book. Ella slammed it shut and scowled at the witch.

'You should've waited to be shown how to use the Book of All Life.'

Seraphina conjured a cigarette out of thin air and slipped it between her purple lips. She dipped her head towards the dragon and winked at it. A tiny puff of flame flickered from the dragon's mouth and lit the ciggy.

'I thought you were that person.'

Ella regained control of her hands and her heart. Seraphina and the dragon and the other Elementals were a new puzzle for her to solve, but she wasn't panicking yet. She could still summon others to help her.

'No, I was never qualified to teach you such wonder.' Seraphina stared at Billy as if he was the main course of her evening meal. 'I know a lot of things about the book, but I can't use it. I'm not special enough for that.'

Confusion crept over Ella's face.

'If it wasn't you who brought these Elementals through the barrier, then who was it?'

'I cannot lie, Ella, for it was I.'

Dora stepped forward and Ella's heart jumped out of her chest.

Seraphina and the dragon bowed their heads together. 'Goddess.'

'Dora... why... how...?' Ella stuttered.

Dora kissed the witch on the chin and stroked the dragon's forehead.

'I'm sorry for the deception, Ella, but once you released me from the book, I had to bide my time and gather my strength. I was weak after centuries of imprisonment, but it's been a privilege seeing how smart and capable you are.'

'I don't understand.'

Ella wanted the floor to open and swallow her. A stabbing pain attacked the back of her head like insects buzzing away inside her brain.

'Think about it, Ella. Who was confined in HIS STORY for allegedly releasing all the evils into the world?'

Dora smiled and Ella sensed millennia of frustration rush into the barn.

'Pandora's Box,' Billy shouted. 'I know all about you.'

Dora's lips crawled to the side of her face.

'Trust the boy to swim in half-truths and falsehoods.' She scowled at him before returning a smile in Ella's direction. 'I think the modern term for it is fake news.'

Dotty stepped forward. 'You're the real Pandora, from mythology?'

Dora performed an exaggerated bow and twirled her hand in the air.

'That is me; also known as the Goddess, Creator of all life.'

Ella wanted to bury her head in the ground.

Daisy glared at Dora. 'God created all life.'

Pandora waved her fingers and dismissed those words into the ether.

'A lie fashioned by men once they'd tricked me into the other realm.' She beamed at Ella. 'I created the book as a doorway back to this world. I didn't consider it would take this long to get into the right hands, but here we are.'

'God is a man,' Daisy protested.

Pandora shook her head. 'Think about what you've just said, child. None of that makes any sense.'

She crept around the barn, her eyes always searching out Ella, who was fascinated and horrified at the same time.

How could I have been so blind?

'What do you mean?' Daisy said.

Pandora stared at Daisy through the gaze of a twelve-year-old girl, but Ella sensed something which had existed for thousands of years.

'In every single species on this planet, who gives birth?'

'Females,' Daisy replied.

'Of course.' Pandora smiled. 'I created females in my image, and everything else came from my imagination. But I was new to creating things on this scale, so there were mistakes. I gave men too much physical strength, but tried to balance it out with emotional weakness. That was a grave error. I made my Elementals special, but there was friction between some of them and humans. I created the other realm to remove the dangerous ones, but then came my biggest blunder.'

Pandora's shoulders slumped, and in that instance, she was just another kid disappointed with the choices she'd made in life.

Ella struggled to come to terms with the reality of the situation. Her friend had betrayed her and it crushed her.

'What did you do?'

'I made the same error many women have for thousands of years. I fell in love with the wrong man, someone who tricked me into banishing myself from this world.' There was a regretful look in Pandora's eyes as she spoke. 'But at least it gave me one good thing in life.'

A sensation of creeping doom engulfed Ella's mind, but she fought the urge to run away.

'What was that?'

'A child,' Pandora replied. 'Who created more children, who themselves brought new life into this world, and on it continued through the centuries as I could only watch from the other side. Until now and...' she stared at Ella, 'you.'

The shivering started in Ella's fingers. She couldn't hold on to the book and it went crashing to the floor. The trembling ran from her wrists and coursed through the rest of her body. Her legs buckled, drawn to the ground as if it was a magnet for flesh. A gloom penetrated her mind and her vision. This was like hearing her parents had disappeared all over again. Her knees cracked into the concrete as her hands fell on either side of the book. Its pages dropped open to the front. Her head bent over, eyes peering into the images of the Elementals she'd summoned to this world.

She dragged her face up and towards Pandora.

'That... that can't be true.'

'How else could you use the book? Only I and those of my bloodline can use it. I called the beasts here while I held your hand and you did your best to repair this damaged realm, which is why their images appeared on the back page.'

Ella didn't want it to be true, but a voice screamed inside her head and said it was. She scraped her knuckles across the ground and watched her blood seep into the concrete.

'Why do this now with me? You've had centuries to find someone else.'

Ella wanted the ground to swallow her up. The duplicity of her friend crushed her soul.

Pandora strode towards the dragon, stroking its chin as it purred at her. She exchanged smiles with Seraphina as Ella got up.

'All the right factors came together with you. The planet's climate is weak enough to create the bridge between worlds and place the book where you found it. Once you opened it in the gateway house, you let me out. All I had to do was bide my time to regain my strength and guide you into what I wanted.'

'You lied, and you manipulated me.'

Anger burst out of Ella, her face burning like volcanic lava. She clutched the pages to her chest.

'You'll forgive me eventually, child, once you've helped me rebuild this world in my image.'

'I want to help you do that.' Dotty walked from the back of the barn and approached Pandora. 'This planet needs to be cleansed.'

Pandora held out her hand, which Dotty took without hesitation.

'I knew you'd be special when Seraphina had her fingers inside your brain at the hospital. You and your sisters are important to me. Dolly, you have strength; Daisy, you have cunning; and Dotty, you have malice.' Pandora gathered them together. 'But I need those qualities in one body. My full power is some time away, but I can still do this.'

She hugged the Twist sisters before pushing them to the side. Yellow light shimmered around her frame before drifting over the cousins and settling on them like a fine mist.

Ella put a trembling hand to her lips.

'What are you doing?'

'Once I'm fully restored, I'll create many wondrous new things and make some significant changes to existing ones.' Pandora grinned at Billy. 'I'll rectify my earlier mistakes, but for now, the Light will do this.'

Her eyes changed colour, yellow sparks glittering inside them.

Dolly, Dotty and Daisy slammed together like sardines in a tin. There was a high-pitched screech as the mist redrew muscle and bone, tearing the sisters apart and putting them back together in a different shape. The three girls became one, taller and wider, hulking over Ella as she gawked in amazement. The combined Twists had bits of the cousins' faces which Ella recognised: Dolly's piercing eyes, Dotty's misshapen nose, and Daisy's curved lips.

'Oh my God,' Billy said.

'Goddess,' Dora said. 'Give me the book, Ella, or your cousin will rip Pudding in half.'

The thing Pandora had created from the Twist girls was unsteady on its new feet, which was unsurprising since they resembled giant slabs of concrete. It swayed from side to side like a massive balloon animal in the wind.

The hybrid creature in front of Ella found its voice.

'I'm gonna murder ya, Smella.'

Ella stumbled backwards, her arm slamming into the wall. Billy froze to the spot. Seraphina laughed and the dragon snarled. Pandora removed the pixie from her pocket and placed it on her shoulder. The thing that was Ella's cousins dragged its brutish hands across the ground and tramped towards her. She twisted her head to find a weapon, but there was nothing.

Before she could lash out in self-defence, the dragon howled in agony. Ella turned as it slumped to the floor and blood flowed from its neck.

'Nooooo,' Seraphina screamed as she ran to the creature. The Irishman's fist caught her face as she slipped in the dragon's blood. The witch hit the ground as he strode forward, the end of his staff covered in red.

He pointed the weapon at Pandora. 'My name is Kylian and I'm here to finish you.'

The Twist abomination grabbed Billy by the throat and lifted him into the air.

Ella crumbled into the dirt.

19 LET THERE BE LIGHT

Billy's legs thrashed in the air as the Twist abomination shook him from side to side.

'Stop!' Ella shouted at the creature that had once been her cousins. Its vast eyes blinked at her while saliva slithered over its chubby lips. It burped loudly enough to shake the dust from the rafters. The stink from its mouth forced her to scowl and put her hand over her face.

Pandora and Seraphina ignored the family disturbance to focus on the young Irishman who'd barged into the barn. Tears dripped from the witch as she knelt next to the slain dragon.

'You bear a remarkable resemblance to the one I loved.' Pandora scrutinised Kylian. 'A simulacrum of the one who betrayed me. It will give me great pleasure to see you eaten alive.'

He twirled the staff in front of him, creating a barrier between them. Seraphina let out a long howl as Ella walked up to Billy's dangling body.

'Listen, Dolly; you don't want to harm Billy.'

The creature hesitated and stared at her. There was a semblance of recognition in its twisted face and she smiled at her mixed-up cousins. And then she remembered all three of them hated her. Now they were joined as one, she could only imagine how much that hate had grown.

'I'm gonna gut ya first, Smella.'

Daisy's voice sent a shiver down Ella's back as the creature dropped Billy. It lunged at her, its long fingers swiping at her face as Billy rolled into the corner. Ella dodged the wrinkled nails and leapt on to the bed. The thing which had once been her cousins stood there confused, staring at its creator for inspiration. Whatever combination of minds existed in that body, they struggled with the movement of its new shape.

Billy ran to Ella. 'We need to get out of here.'

'Return the book to the portal, Ella,' Kylian said as he kept a watchful eye on Pandora and Seraphina. 'Send the creatures back to the other realm and seal the book where you found it.' He inched away from the glaring eyes of the witch, keeping the shaft spinning as a barrier between those that threatened him. He made his way to Ella as Pandora consoled Seraphina. The Twist abomination was rooted to the spot, looking confused about what it should do. Its hulk of a body swayed from side to side.

Kylian held out his free arm towards Ella, his gaze fixed on his enemy. 'Take the bracelet from my wrist.'

'Why?'

Ella's vision switched from him and Pandora, drifting between them to peer at the hole the dragon had made in the barn. It was the only way out, but they'd have to get past Pandora, Seraphina and the hulking mixed-up creature to reach it.

'Place the book with this and seal them in the container where you found it. That will return her to the other realm.'

Ella hesitated, unsure if she should believe him. She glanced over at the dragon he'd killed before taking the bracelet and staring at him.

Should I trust him after what happened between us on the beach? Is he another one to betray me?

'I'm the last of my line, the only one who can stop her.' Kylian spoke to Ella, but his vision stayed on Pandora. 'If I'm stopped and you don't send her back, you'll need an army of monsters to defeat her.'

'Not all Elementals are terrible.' Ella knew this from her recent experiences.

'You're naïve and out of your depth, child.' The bitterness in his voice saddened her.

'What will you do?' She noticed Pandora whispering into the mangled ear of her latest creation.

'I'll keep these things away from you.'

'Why should I trust you?'

Kylian held the staff in front of him as the Twist abomination swayed on its feet. Pandora stroked its brutish hand and it lurched for them. It emitted a foul smell as it strode forward.

'Go now,' Kylian said as the creature leapt. The Twist sisters hit the Irishman in their new conjoined form as he pushed the weapon towards the creature's huge head. They landed in a lump on the ground.

Ella jumped from the bed and over the top of them as they rolled in the dirt. Billy followed her as they faced their former friend. Seraphina was sprawled across the dragon, shedding a waterfall of tears over the dead Elemental. Pandora stood between them and their escape.

'I need that book, Ella.' Her voice was cruel and

primeval, transforming Dora's innocent twelve-year-old face into something which had suffered an aeon's worth of torment. There were deep wrinkles embedded into her skin, which had lost its youthful vigour and replaced it with a grey sheen reminiscent of ancient paper. Dora's once luxurious blonde hair had transformed into Pandora's raggedy white locks.

She ran her fingers over her cheek and sighed. 'I expended too much Light melding your cousins together.' Her words were brittle and a little broken. 'If you share your Light with me, I'll be right as rain in a jiffy.'

Pandora sprang at her, grabbing hold of Ella's shoulder as she tried to shield the book. Pandora had her arms around Ella as the two of them bundled into Billy. They all went tumbling like dominoes. As they hit the ground, the Twist abomination tossed Kylian across the barn.

'Let go of me,' Ella shouted.

'You're my kin, Ella; we should work together.' Pandora pinned her into the cold concrete and her breath spread over Ella's face. Ella weakened as Pandora absorbed Light from her. 'The connection between us is making me stronger.'

Pandora's head lit up like a shooting star, her skin shining brightly enough to illuminate the barn. She was young again as Ella stared into the eyes of the girl she'd thought her friend.

'You're killing me, Dora.' Ella's voice shuddered, her gaze glued to Pandora. The Goddess dithered, appearing to understand the seriousness of what she was doing. The hesitation helped Ella. She remembered how she'd taken Light from Star, reaching in her mind for that connection to Pandora and pushing it in the other direction. 'Oh my goodness.'

Light from Pandora streamed into her, but it differed from what she'd felt from the unicorn; this was prehistoric and powerful. Strength returned to her bones and her body trembled with energy.

'No.' Despair consumed Pandora's face. Ella seized the opportunity, pushing Pandora back and sending her into the foot of the bed. Billy grabbed hold of Ella's arm and dragged her up. Ella gazed at Pandora, feeling more alive than ever before.

A shrieking howl drew her attention away. She stared at the thing which had once been her cousins as it ran into the shadows where it had sent the Irishman. It shrieked something unnatural as Pandora laughed at Ella.

'You'd like to make the world a better place and so would I.'

Pandora climbed on to the bed and pushed her arms out.

'You want to rule the world.' Ella held Billy's arm. The only thing between them and escape from the barn was Seraphina. Ella kept one eye on Pandora while glancing at the witch. Seraphina's body convulsed with sobs as she lay on top of the dragon. 'You'll kill those who don't agree with you.' There was steel inside Ella's voice, which surprised even her. Pandora dropped her arms and stared at her with disappointment dripping from those ancient eyes.

'You say this when you've allied yourself with those that hate me, one of whose agents killed that beautiful creature behind you.'

Pandora pointed at the dragon and the distraught witch. There was a pain in Ella's heart for what the Irishman had done. She had to put that to the side if she were to undo all the horror Pandora had released into the world.

Billy squeezed her hand.

'I don't trust you, Dora, not anymore.' She pictured their escape route and knew what she had to do. 'I'll save this world and the Elementals my way.'

Pandora shook her head and groaned.

'You've inherited my stubbornness, child.'

She stepped down from the bed and strode towards them.

'You go, Ella,' Billy said. 'I'll handle her.'

Pandora cackled. 'I may be weakened, boy, but I'll gobble you up and consume your Light.'

Billy's fingers trembled in Ella's hand, but she was calm.

'I'll give you the book.' Ella was stony-faced as Pandora looked surprised. 'All you had to do was ask.'

Billy was ashen-faced as Pandora stepped forward. Ella removed the book from her pocket and smiled at the girl who had once been her friend. Pandora's eyes lit up with glee as Ella swung her arm in an arc and smashed her on the side of her head. The Goddess hit the ground and screamed. It was a loud, unnatural shriek that was thousands of years old.

'Run!' Ella shouted as she let go of Billy.

They clambered over the body of the dragon and ran from the barn. Wind and rain battered them as they got outside. Billy was next to Ella as they headed for the path along the cliffs and Pandora howled.

'What now?' Billy yelled.

'We have to get to the safety of the mystery house.'

Ella glanced over her shoulder to see if Pandora had followed them. There was guilt in her heart for leaving the Irishman with the Twist monstrosity. She hoped his plan for the book and the bracelet would save him, and her cousins would return to normal.

Thunder screeched above them as she sprinted as fast as

she could. In her mind, Ella saw those terrible images from the television, of the Elementals Pandora had brought to the world which now terrorised the country. She wanted to stop running and take the book and send those dreadful things back, but there wasn't time: they needed the safety of the mystery house first.

The noise in the air grew louder and she expected lightning to flash around them at any second. She peered into the sky as she ran. There were no streaks of light there, only a dark shadow falling on her. Her eyes adjusted to the gloom as a screaming beast dived at her. Its outstretched claws caught Ella on the cheek. She fell into the grass, her body rolling towards the edge of the cliff.

'Ella!' Billy roared as she tasted blood and dirt at the back of her throat.

The harpy circled above them and prepared to dive again. A spine-chilling screech escaped from its mouth as it lunged and scraped its talons across Ella's leg. Yellowed nails cut into her jeans, but not far enough to pierce her skin. The monster pulled upwards and hovered above them.

Then it dived once more.

The book was tucked into Ella's trousers, its cover sticking into her flesh. As the creature attacked, she whipped it from her pocket and swung her arm into the sky. She struck the harpy across its twisted face and sent it tumbling towards the sea.

'Come on.' Billy pulled her up. 'I'll slow it down.' She saw the brick in his fingers. 'You get to the house and destroy that book.'

She looked into his pale eyes as the shriek rose over the cliffs. Billy dashed to the harpy and crashed the stone into its head. Ella pushed away her fears for him and sprinted towards the building. The bracelet was in one hand, the book in the other. Something unnatural was behind her, breathing at her flesh as she ran for her life. She didn't glance back, her heart ready to eat through her libs.

The mystery house was just in front of her as icy fingers touched her neck.

Ella burst through the door and slammed it shut. The book and bracelet tumbled to the floor as Star purred at her. She ignored the unicorn and ran to the window. She couldn't see Billy or the harpy anywhere. A chill rippled through her neck, but there was no sign of whatever had reached out for her.

'Oh, Billy.' Ella put her hands on her face. 'What have I done to you?'

She collapsed and cried a sea of tears. She'd abandoned the Irishman in the barn and left Billy to fight for his life on the cliffs. As much as she disliked her cousins, she felt guilty because of what Dora had done to them.

Not Dora; Pandora.

She looked to the window. Outside, dragons swooped through the sky and headed for the town. Guilt swept through Ella like a tsunami for every terrible thing that had happened and was still to come.

All she could do now was save Billy and Kylian. She crawled on her hands and knees towards the book. Pain shot through her legs and dust swirled in her face. She grabbed it from the floor and turned to the back. The illustrations of the monstrous Elementals burnt into her eyes.

How could I have been so stupid with Dora? I should've known what she was doing.

Her shoulders ached as she peered into the images. She placed her palm over the pictures and focused on them. Ella cleared her head of pain, of the guilt, and concentrated on one task only.

'Return to where you came from. Go back to the other realm.'

She repeated the words for a minute. She imagined each of those dangerous Elementals vanishing from the world and returning to the other side. She felt the outline of the pictures underneath her skin, so she pressed down further and harder until all that was there was blank paper. When she moved her fingers away, the pages were empty once again.

She sat back and sighed with relief.

I hope that's saved you, Billy, you and the rest of the world.

She turned to the front of the book and placed one finger over the image of the witch. Should she keep her promise? Seraphina had betrayed her, so why should she stick to her word? She owed the witch nothing. It would serve her right to return to the realm she hated so much.

'Think before you do anything, Ella.'

Pain shot through her chest as she turned. Pandora stood in the open doorway, the wind spinning around her as fire and electricity lit up the atmosphere. Dragons roared and sirens screeched as they disappeared from the sky. The air stank of smoke as it drifted into the house.

Pandora closed the door and scrutinised Ella. She'd grown young once more and was the Dora Ella had befriended in the last couple of days. The betrayal stabbed at her heart again.

'You lied from the start.'

Ella's fingers dug into the book and she was tempted to spring forward and thump her former friend. Pandora shook her head, that youthful expression betrayed by the experience beaming from her eyes.

'It was a necessary deception, but I am sorry.'

Ella gazed into Pandora's eyes. 'You trapped me like a spider tempting a fly, and all because you want to destroy the world. The centuries you've spent in the other realm have made you bitter and twisted.'

Pandora shrugged and pouted at Ella.

'If I'd told you who I was, explained my story, would you have believed me? Would you have understood the connection we have?'

It was Ella's turn to shake her head.

'I trusted you with my life. I thought we were friends.'

She moved towards Star, her mind ticking over with what to do.

'We are much more than that, Ella. You know this to be true because we're family.'

The pixie on Pandora's shoulder danced a little jig and fluttered its wings. Ella guessed the small Elemental was feeding off the Light coursing through Pandora, who appeared to be stronger inside the mystery house.

'I have no family anymore.' She fought back the tears as she remembered her parents.

Is that it? Have I given up all faith in finding them?

Pandora ran her fingers over the pixie's delicate gossamer wings.

'You remind me so much of my daughter, Hope.' Sadness engulfed her voice. 'I had to observe from the other side as she grew into a fine young woman; watch as she died in the realm of men when I could have kept her alive for all eternity. And on it went for centuries as my descendants, always women and girls, suffered in the world I'd created. You don't know how the guilt continues to burn inside me.'

She clenched one fist as the pixie shivered in the other palm.

'I'm sorry, Dora.' Ella deliberately used her other name. 'Sorry for all the terrible things that happened to you and your family, but none of that excuses the chaos you've unleashed.'

Pandora was indifferent to Ella's words. 'We have the chance to make this world a much better place.'

'Make the planet a better place by killing people?' Ella sneered. 'I've heard that before.'

'Yes,' Pandora replied. 'That is the overriding lesson from history. I blame myself for the oppression and genocide committed in this world. That's why I'm here to rectify my mistakes.' There was no wavering in her voice. 'You're a clever girl, Ella; you must realise the world can't continue like this, driven by greed and hate. Look at what humans have done to the planet and all the other life on it. At this rate, there'll be no living thing left here within fifty years.'

Ella understood the determination written across Pandora's face, recognised the conviction in her voice. But she'd spent the time listening to Pandora to reinforce her resolve. She'd set her plan and there was no changing from it.

She placed the bracelet on the book and held it over the box where she'd found those pages.

Courage gripped her heart.

'If I seal this inside here, will you disappear into the other realm?'

Pandora removed the pixie from her shoulder and placed it on the unicorn.

'All the other Elementals will go with me.' Pandora stroked Star. 'The creatures busy repairing the damage to the planet's environment will vanish. There'll be no hope left for this world.' She peered through the window.

'That's better than handing it over to you.' The tips of Ella's fingers shook.

'You know, it's only a matter of time before man destroys everything here. The barrier will collapse, and I and all the others will return to reign over the ruins. Sealing the book in the box is like putting a band-aid over a terminal wound.'

She made no move to approach Ella; didn't attempt to take the book from her hand.

'Kylian said if I destroyed the book, that would stop you.'

'Do you trust the Irish boy?' Ella wasn't sure what to believe. 'Even if it were possible, destroying it wouldn't end me. All you'd do is kill every other Elemental, all the good and the bad. And then I'd just create more.'

Ella accepted the truth in Pandora's words. Sending her back now would drive all the others with her. The challenge was how to save the planet without ending it at the same time.

'Not all humans are terrible.' Ella expected the book to shake in her hand, but she was as steady as a rock. 'There's more good in the world than bad.'

She'd lost her parents, been forced to live with a family who hated her and who only wanted her for money. She'd been bullied at school, but still believed most people were decent, kind and honest. She wouldn't let a minority twist the way she saw life.

'It only takes one bad human to infect the others.' Pandora stroked the head of the unicorn as she spoke. 'Humanity is a disease of my making and I need to rectify my mistake.' The pixie lay on Star's back and snored, its tiny wings vibrating along with the sounds. 'We can do this together, you and me. We either fix everything now or wait until things get much, much worse. And the longer you hesitate, the harder it will be to correct the devastation done to the environment. And more people will die.'

'What will you do?' Ella opened the box. Something tugged at her heart and she wondered if she'd collapse.

'Balance needs to be restored to this realm. With my guidance and your help, some Elementals will restore the right amount of Light to the world, while others will ensure the crimes of humans never happen again.'

'How will you do that?'

The book felt heavy in Ella's hand. The bracelet was underneath vibrating on top of it.

'I'll take charge and deal with any who stand in my way. There'll be no mistakes on my part this time. My eyes and heart will be a wall to all deception.'

Mania bristled inside Pandora's glittering eyes.

'You sound like a bully.' Ella lowered her hand into the box.

Pandora stared at her. 'It's your only real choice.'

'No, it isn't.' Ella dropped the bracelet and the book into the box, holding the lid in her other hand. 'In the myth, it wasn't a box you opened, was it?'

All those times her mother had encouraged her to read,

to study history and the great mythologies returned at that moment. She remembered the story of Pandora's Box and the young woman whose curiosity got the better of her and who supposedly released all the evils into the world.

Pandora smiled at her. 'I created a Juxtaposed Analogous Realm where the most dangerous Elementals could live without harming humanity.' She waved a wistful arm in the air. 'I'd forgotten that the most dangerous one of all was me. It was enough for the one I loved to trick me into banishment.' Sorrow washed out of her. 'I lost my world, my creations, and my daughter.'

'So now you want your revenge?'

'It's not about revenge, Ella. It's about rectifying my mistakes and healing the wounds of this planet.'

She needed more time to make the right decision.

'How long will it take the Elementals to fix the environment?'

Pandora shrugged. 'They could correct the damage done to nature in a year. But it will mean little if humans continue to pollute the world; which they will. The only logical solution is mine.'

Ella struggled with what to do. She didn't trust Pandora, but if she sealed the book and sent all the Elementals back to the other realm, there would be no saving the environment.

She had to sacrifice something; but what?

'I don't believe you.'

'I can sweeten the deal for you.'

Pandora lifted the sleeping pixie from Star and placed it on her shoulder like a pirate with a parrot. Her grin unnerved Ella.

'More tricks and lies from you?'

'This will be the greatest truth for you, Ella; the answer to your biggest mystery.'

Ella's hand throbbed. It was a pain that transferred to her heart with what Pandora implied.

'You mean...?'

'I can return your parents to you.'

Ella's legs swayed, electricity shooting through every part of her. Lightning flashed outside and burnt into the front of her head.

'What... how...?'

'It wasn't my first choice of action, I have to admit.' The pixie was awake on Pandora's shoulder, its sleepy eyes darting around the room. 'I'd hoped to use your mother for this, but she was too old and too stuck in her science to believe creatures from myth and superstition existed. Even when I poked a few of the smaller Elementals through the gap between worlds into her laboratory, she shrugged them off as aberrations in human or animal biology. I'd used most of my strength, creating the doorway on the cliffs, so I had to place your parents in a holding location in your world. They're safe, but I could end that with one word.'

'You took my mum and dad?' Ella struggled to come to terms with the idea.

'It had to be done. The nexus for the gateway is in that one specific space. The only way I could think of getting you there was by having you live with your cousins. That's when your parents became expendable. But I can bring them back to you. They're still in this realm, being looked after by some of my most loyal subjects.'

The lid lay heavily in Ella's hand. She wanted to leave, to drop it and see Pandora disappear forever, but the thought of seeing her parents again had thrown her plan out the window.

'You're lying.' But she knew it to be true.

'You can have them back and save the environment if you agree to work with me. We will end all war; eradicate suffering, oppression, hunger, poverty and all the other cruelties invented by humans.'

She inched her way closer to Ella.

'No.' Ella placed the lid halfway over the box. If she let go, it would be all over, but she'd lose her parents forever. 'I have a different suggestion.'

Pandora's lips twitched. 'I'm listening.'

Ella pushed the lid down until it covered most of the box.

'If you return to the other realm for five years, I'll work with you when you come back.'

Only a slither of light escaped from the box as she spoke.

'Why should I do that?' Pandora asked.

'That's plenty of time to restore the damage to the climate and allow me to educate humanity about what's been hidden from them since your imprisonment.' Ella did her best to play on Pandora's vanity. 'You can't expect humans to accept you just like that; all of what you told me will come as a shock to people. If you give me five years, I'll pave the way for your arrival when I tell everyone what happened and how the others betrayed you. You'll have millions of followers ready for your return. I'll make sure all of that happens when I show people what I can do with the book.'

Pandora stared at the top of the box. 'And what if I refuse?'

'Then I'll close this, imprisoning you on the other side.'

Ella summoned all of her courage and strength into her words.

Pandora smirked and stroked the pixie's head.

'With the damage already done to the climate, the barrier will weaken enough for me to return. All you'd do is delay the inevitable.'

'That could be centuries from now, and I'll ensure the world is ready to resist you. Instead of telling people of your betrayal, I'll make sure they see you as a monster waiting to destroy us all. The world knows Elementals exist now. It won't be hard for me to convince everyone you're to blame.'

Pandora scratched her chin and squinted at Ella. The twelve-year-old girl was gone, replaced by something older than time.

'I think you would, descendant of mine.'

The pixie jumped from her shoulder and ran across the floor, chasing something only it saw. Pandora stared at it in silent contemplation.

Ella's arm ached. If Pandora didn't agree to her terms, she didn't know what she'd do.

Save the world from Pandora or save my parents?

Pandora held a hand out to her. 'I agree to your demands. Shall we shake on it?'

Ella ignored the gesture. There was one more thing she needed.

'You must return my mum and dad.'

The thought of seeing them again clouded her mind,

but she fought through the confusion to stay focused on her plan.

'You drive a hard bargain. You remind me of me.'

Pandora stretched out her hand, her immaculate nails working like scissors to slice through the space in front of her, using her fingers to cut a hole in the air. An electric surge rippled through the room, yellow and white light burning in the air. The house smelt of fried apples as she grinned at Ella.

Pandora reached inside the gap she'd conjured out of nothing and pulled Ella's parents out one by one.

Ella dropped the lid to the floor and ran to them.

'Mum!' She threw her arms around her mother. Gemma Finn was bleary-eyed and confused. 'Dad!' Ella stretched her body as far as she could to include her father. She hugged them for an eternity before lifting her tear-stained face. Pandora closed the hole and created another one. Ella knew it was a door to the Elemental realm.

Pandora stepped halfway into the gap.

'I'll see you in five years.'

Pandora's mischievous smile disappeared into the other world.

'I need a drink,' Ella's dad said as he held hands with his wife and child.

Gemma Finn kissed her daughter as the three of them moved to the door. Ella turned towards the box, scooping out the book and the bracelet the Irishman had given her. She owed him her life. And she had to find Billy.

Andrew Finn pointed to the book. 'What's that?'

'We've got a lot to talk about, Dad.' Ella led them out of the mystery house. 'But I have to find my friend first.' The joy of seeing her parents again was outweighed by what might have happened to Billy. 'I'll be back for you two later.' Ella closed the door on Star and the pixie.

'Billy!' she shouted to the boy sitting outside. Ella let go of her mother's hand and jumped on top of him.

'Mind me bruised bones.' He laughed as they tumbled on the grass.

'I thought you were gone,' she said when they came up for air.

'It takes more than a crazed woman with rotten teeth and terrible fingernails to get rid of me. Otherwise, me ma would have done it years ago.'

There were cuts to his forehead and dried blood on his cheeks. The harpy had ripped half of his shirt away.

'Where are we, Ella?' Gemma raised her fingers to her face. 'I remember being at work, and then nothing.'

The northeastern wind blew across them as Ella stared towards the Twist home in the distance. She had to take her parents and Billy to safety.

'Come on.' Ella grabbed her mother's hand in hers. 'Let's get cleaned up and something to eat and I'll tell you everything.'

They talked little on the way to the house, a sense of relief pouring from all of them. Ella's mum and dad were in a daze as if they'd been in a deep sleep for the last six months.

'What about the Twist sisters?' Billy was nervous as they reached the barn.

There was a spade outside the door and Ella picked it up as she pushed her way in, ready for the thing which used to be her cousins.

'Dolly?' She searched for the light switch and called out for her cousin. There was no sign of the creature or the Irishman who'd saved their lives. The dragon and the other

Elementals were gone. But an old friend was sitting on the bed. 'Ratter!' She dropped the spade and ran to the little rodent, lifting Ratter in her hands and grinning at her hairy face.

'What is this place?' Gemma Finn stared at the bed and the other domestic appliances.

Ella placed Ratter on her shoulder. 'Aunt Ida said I had to sleep in here.'

'Did she now?' Gemma Finn's face twisted into an unpleasant shape. 'I think I need to have a word with my sister.'

They trooped out of the barn and into the house. An eerie silence greeted them, shattered by Ella's foot crunching on the broken ornament on the floor. It was one of Aunt Ida's porcelain dolls, arms and legs strewn across the ground.

The living room door was open. Ella strode past the others and barged through. A few days ago, she had been scared every time she stepped into this place, but now she was fearless.

The home was a mess, with broken furniture scattered everywhere. Someone had smashed a large olive-green lamp through the centre of the TV. A battle had been waged there, but there was no sign of who'd done so much damage.

Ella stared at her parents. Weariness seeped out of them as shadows darker than the night overtook their faces. Ella put her hand on her mother's arm and guided her to the sofa.

'You and Dad get some rest while Billy and I check the house.' They didn't protest as Ella led Billy into the kitchen, greeted with a similar scene of upturned furniture and broken utensils. The upstairs rooms were free of damage and people. The Twist family were gone.

Ella took responsibility and steered her parents into the largest of the bedrooms. 'Get some sleep, and I'll see you later.' She hugged them both.

'Goodnight,' Gemma Finn said to her daughter.

'Goodbye.' Ella closed the door behind her. She ran downstairs and into the kitchen to find Billy stuffing his face with a sandwich. 'You don't waste any time.' She ignored her own hunger.

'I'm starving.' He talked through a mouthful of cheese and bread. Ella grabbed it from his hand and took a bite from it.

'Ugh! What is that?' Ella turned and spat into the sink.

'It's strong French cheese.' Billy giggled as he spoke. Ella wiped her mouth and sat opposite him. She placed the book on the table and he lost his smile when he saw it. 'It's not over, is it?'

'No.' Ella told him about the arrangement she'd made with Pandora.

'So, she'll be back in five years?' He finished the food with a frown.

'Not quite,' Ella replied. 'You forget that time flows differently there. One day there is eight days here.' She tried not to laugh as he struggled to work out the calculations.

'So, that means...'

'One year in the other realm is eight years here. If Pandora keeps her word, she won't be back for forty years.' She'd made sure the figures were right before offering the deal to Pandora. Billy sighed with relief and wiped a stray piece of cheese from his chin. 'Forty years to prepare the world for her return, to tell people the real story of Pandora.'

'How will you do that?'

Ella stood and pushed the book towards him.

'I won't. You'll help my parents do it.' She moved from

the table and towards the door. 'I've sent the good Elementals back for now, until the world understands what they are.'

Billy made a massive circle with his open mouth. She held her hands out and felt the energy in her flesh.

'I didn't believe it at first, that Pandora is my ancestor, but I know the truth now.' Ella let the Light flow through her, the oomph settling at the top of her fingers. She used her index finger to draw a line vertically in front of her. 'Her Light lives in me now.'

'What are you going to do, Ella?'

'I can't just wait here and let Pandora return. The book will give you access to the invisible house. When I can, I'll bring Elementals to you. I need to prepare an army from the other side and transport it here.'

Ella slipped one arm and leg through the gap she'd created between this realm and the other one. She smiled at Billy.

'A few days ago, I had nothing but loneliness and the fear of what was inside this place. Now I have my parents back and a new friend.' There were tears in Billy's eyes as she spoke. 'Now, I have the strength to save two worlds.'

With those words, Ella Finn disappeared.

THANK YOU!

Thank you, dear reader for purchasing this book.

If you enjoyed reading about Ella Finn her journey continues in these books:

Ella and the Elementals
Ella and the Multiverse
Ella and the Monsters
Ella and the Dreamers

Many thanks to my wonderful wife for all her support and patience.

A big thank you to Lara Crawley for letting me use her name in this book - and to her parents, Anna and Garry for agreeing to this.

Extra special thanks to Karina Gallagher for being a dedicated reader of my work.

Ella and the Elementals edited by Alison Jack.

Cover design by James, GoOnWrite.com

ABOUT THE AUTHOR

Andrew French lives amongst faded seaside glamour on the North East coast of England. He likes gin and cats but not together, new music and old movies, curry and ice cream. Slow bike rides and long walks to the pub are his usual exercise, as well as flicking through the pages of good books and the memoirs of bad people.

Find out more at www.andrewsfrench.com

Facebook:

https://www.facebook.com/A-S-French-Author-150145625006018

Twitter:

www.twitter.com/andrewfrench100

Instagram:

www.instagram.com/andrewfrench100

And replies to all his email at mail@andrewsfrench.com

If you have the time, please leave a review at Amazon or Goodreads

Thank you!